Bonners' Fairy, by Elizabeth Patterson, has been one of the most entertaining books I've had the gift of reading. At no time did I find it slow. The book was a page-turner from the very beginning.

Charming, imaginative, and the only thing that could possibly make it better is the release of the next book soon. Very impressive.

—*Robert White*

I read the book, and I loved it. My favorite part was when Haley and Henry first got into Roan. I loved all the characters and the way you described things; you made me really want to taste rainbow dew. Anyway, I love the book. I think that a lot of people are going to like it too.
P.S. I loved the note that you wrote me in the book.

—*Jessica Kirk, age 11*

This fascinating tale tells of Haley and Henry and their childhood escapades into the land of the fairies to save Zeb from the obsidian stone of Molock.

I thoroughly enjoyed this tale and eagerly await to hear more from our young heroes!

—*Sherwin Bydens, award-winning producer, professional actor*

I met Elizabeth at a book signing and was delighted to get her book. I had no idea how fun it would be to read! I thought it would be more of a tween book, but it appealed as an adult as well.

I would highly recommend it for all ages. What a fun tale of adventure and intrigue! Great book!

—*Gina Geldbach-Hall, author of* Firegal . . . Rising from the Ashes

A whimsical and uplifting fairytale for the future. A colorful and magical story of hope for all generations. It is a very comforting read for one's imagination that will leave you wanting more. A story to read and share with the whole family.

—*Sean Crawford*

Children of all ages will enjoy this story, for it is a compelling story of good over evil and courage and love over fear and hate.

A New Kind of Battle is the second book in a series by Elizabeth Rymer Patterson. Her first was a spell-binding and wonderful story I couldn't put down. *A New Kind of Battle* is just as wonderful, and again, I couldn't put it down. Elizabeth is a fantastic storyteller with characters so vivid and awesome that you are drawn into their world and lives. I can't wait for book three. I have known Elizabeth for years and never knew she had this kind of talent and imagination. I have a new respect and love for her. Keep writing, Elizabeth; you are amazing.

—Sally Meyer, South Lake Tahoe, CA

Just when Haley and her twin brother Henry return from their amazing adventure in Roan, a land of fairies, Sersha, their dear friend and fairy princess, returns to the human world with news of trouble. Haley and Henry set off immediately to the breathtaking and enchanted world to help explain the dangerous and mysterious happenings in the normally peaceful realm. Things that seem to come so easily for humans aren't so easy for fairies, and now, with the help of Haley and Henry, they have to learn how to live with the beautiful chaos that emotions can bring.

Bonners' Fairy: A New Kind of Battle sweeps you off into an enchanted world of fairies that can change size with a snap, witches on broomsticks, mermaids with beautiful shimmering tails, and creatures beyond imagination. Patterson's intricate details paint the picture of the captivating world of Roan so well that you feel as though you are flying through the air with Haley, taking in the breathtaking sights or talking to the Bocan Fish at Julius Caesar's house. It makes you believe that fairytales can be true and wish on that falling star that you can explore the world with your own eyes. *Bonners' Fairy: A New Kind of Battle* takes you to that world.

—Wendy Lee, Gardnerville, NV

Patterson does it again, *Sailing Toward Destiny,* bringing childhood characters to life and showing us how the bonds of love and friendship can conquer the most difficult of challenges. She displays how a scary and impossible journey to find and kill Medusa can be accomplished with the help of friends and loved ones. It's a great book and a must read series; can't wait for the next one!

—Wendy Martin, South Lake Tahoe, CA

I really like the *Bonners' Fairy* books. They are exciting, very good stories, and I really get into them. I'll keep spreading the word on your books!

—*Rain Allsenberrie, Nevada*

This series is magical! I became lost in this fantasy world and didn't want to put the books down. Elizabeth has a way of captivating the reader. I was entranced by the entire series and cannot wait till the next one comes out!

—*Dena LeGross, Nevada*

I finished the first book of the *Bonners' Fairy* series. It was quite the read! Elizabeth Patterson wrote her first book in a way that causes the reader to want more. She is a very creative individual and I enjoy her storytelling. I cannot wait to read the rest of the series!

—*Addison Poulin, Maine*

Bonners' Fairy

A NEW KIND OF BATTLE

Elizabeth Rymer Patterson

Published by
Elizabeth Rymer Patterson

Production Team
Patricia Beaulieu, Literary Agent, book division manager, and editor; Nancy Ratkiewich, book production, njr productions; Juliette Burns, cover designer; David Patterson, author photographer Elizabeth Rymer Patterson

For general information on other products and services, please visit the website: https://www.bonnersfairy.com/

ISBN: 979-8-9897207-2-9 Paperback
ISBN: 979-8-9897207-3-6 eBook

LCCN: 2012908347

Printed in the United States of America

Dedication

For my beautiful mother,
Dorothy Belle

Contents

Acknowledgments

Gratitude and love goes to my husband, David, for unwavering support throughout this journey.

I extend heartfelt thanks to Trish Beaulieu, not only my Literary Agent but also my editor and proofreader. Your invaluable contributions have played a pivotal role in shaping this work.

Special acknowledgment goes to Nancy Ratkiewich, the driving force behind the book's production, who handled the layout and formatting with utmost precision. Your dedication is vital to the readers who are engaging with this material.

A sincere shout-out to Juliette Burns, the creative mind behind the captivating cover design. Your imaginative prowess has exceeded all expectations, adding a unique and compelling dimension to the project.

Most of all, I thank the Lord. Without Him, this story would never have evolved into such an adventure.

When we last left Haley and her twin, they retired wearily to bed,

planning to visit the courtyard portal in the morning. However, their

rest was abruptly shattered as a window in Haley's room crashed

open, revealing a battered and injured Sersha. With desperate

urgency, she pleaded for their return, mentioning trouble and the

name Valian before collapsing, her damaged wing

resembling a snapped branch.

A LONG WAIT

June was normally hot in Bonners Ferry, Idaho, even in the mountains, but it was a cool morning around forty degrees. It was raining lightly, and you could smell the dirt as the drops hit the ground. Autumn birds had arrived early and were nestled in the trees, cackling to each other. They were the same birds Haley Miles looked forward to hearing in late September.

Her windows were open to let in the fresh air, making the room chilly, but the crackling fire in the old pot-bellied stove always brought a warm feeling of contentment.

She looked over at the figure lying asleep in her bed and pondered the events of the last few hours.

Sersha was a fairy princess who lived in a palace in the city of Roan, in a land called Wisen. It existed in another realm. Fairies could enter the human world through a portal invisible to the human eye. Sersha arrived at Haley's bedroom window, battered and bruised, then collapsed, but as she slept, she began to mend as Manwan fairies have the ability to heal themselves whenever they are injured.

Disguised to look human with their fairy wings shrouded by magic, Sersha and Valian first appeared to Haley and her twin brother, Henry, at the annual autumn festival in the small town of Bonners Ferry. Sersha and her blonde-haired, blue-eyed, very muscular brother, Prince Valian, were desperate for help in rescuing Zeb Bonner. He was their friend and also the founder of Haley's hometown, a human who disappeared almost two hundred years ago and wound up in the fairy world. An evil presence they called Molock the Merciless held him captive. The twins accepted the challenge and helped rescue not only Zeb but also his wife Sarah and his daughters, Susan and Rosie, who had also disappeared from Bonners Ferry, presumed lost in the Kootenai River.

Haley and her family lived on the old Bonner homestead, and Haley's resemblance to Zeb's wife, Sarah, was uncanny. They were each petite and almost identical with thick, long, dark hair and very beautiful, and both loved adventure.

When Sersha first saw Haley, she just knew that Haley would be able to help.

When Haley and Henry first entered the fairy world, they met up with Prince Valian. He gave them an elixir, which caused them to grow wings and also produced something called a dwindle drop, which looked like a frozen water droplet. After the twins ate their drops, they were able to shrink in size to mere inches in height. Later, Valian's mother, Queen Lilia, bestowed upon each of them a shroud so they could hide their wings when necessary.

Haley sat and watched Sersha as she slept. She was frantic at what could have happened in the short time she and Henry had been home from Wisen.

Sersha finally stirred and rolled over just before sunrise. She turned and looked at Haley. Tears began to roll down her cheeks as she sat up.

"What happened to you? How did you get hurt?" Haley asked with concern.

Sersha took a deep breath and began to recount everything she could remember.

"After you and Henry left Roan, Valian and I went into the Spicewood realm with several other guardians. Word had come that moss trolls had been spotted heading toward the palace, so we went to check it out. We were only about twenty miles in when it happened," she sobbed.

"What?" Haley asked, alarmed.

"We were ambushed, completely taken by surprise! We didn't even see them until they were right on top of us. Boar trolls! Nearly everyone was injured, and we barely escaped. I was hit across my wing and could hardly fly. The other guardians had to help me; otherwise, I would not have gotten away."

She paused for a moment, trying to recall every bit of information she could.

"Something happened . . . Valian was . . . stabbed . . . he . . . he . . . "

"Stabbed?" Haley whispered.

"He's alive . . . " Sersha quickly reassured her, "he's alive, but . . . "

"But what?" Haley asked, her voice trembling.

"He's not healing! He's not healing, and we don't know why!"

"I need to go to him," Haley said, unveiling her wings.

They jumped from Haley's west tower bedroom window and flew to the portal next to the old oak tree in the courtyard.

They waited for the glittering tower to appear, marking the entrance. Nothing happened. Haley had lost the ruby necklace she found, which Sersha told her was the key for a human to see a portal. Sersha didn't need a key; she could see them on her own, but she was having no luck either.

"I don't understand," said Sersha. "I know portals move around, but I should be able to see it."

They gave each other worried looks.

When the twins first moved onto the Bonner homestead, they found what they thought was a treasure map. Later, Sersha told them the map marked the portals to what Estelle, their housekeeper, referred to as "the other side." They were also able to see more portals on the map that were invisible to humans, except for Haley. They were revealed to her when she put the necklace on.

"Let's try another portal," Haley suggested.

They flew off to the old swimming hole but could not find that entrance or any other. They arrived back at the Miles family estate, worried and confused.

So here she was once again, another new morning, standing at one of the windows of her room, looking out at the valley below. She found herself there often, daydreaming, wishing she was back in Roan.

She glanced over at Sersha, asleep in her bed. She was such a beautiful fairy. Her long auburn hair was as soft as the breast of a dove. She gave off an aurora of gentle kindness and harmony, yet she was vulnerable being out of her element. She slept almost the entire time since she arrived, and Haley was worried about her being gone from home for too long.

Her thoughts dwelt on Valian. Was he still hurt? Was he in danger? Did he know that Sersha was trapped on *this side?* Was he trying to find a way to open the portals? She had deep feelings for him and felt that she was falling in love with him. She saw his rugged face in her dreams and could see affection in his pale blue eyes when he looked at her. It gave her a warm feeling in her belly, and she wondered if that was what it felt like to be in love.

She stoked the fire in the stove and stared out at the low-lying clouds, lost in recent memories.

She heard a shuffling outside her door and quickly drew the curtains around her four-poster bed.

"Who's there?" she whispered.

"It's me," Henry answered.

With a sigh of relief, she opened the door. Henry walked in, followed closely by Estelle. Haley looked at Henry questioningly.

"It's alright," Estelle said, quietly walking over to the bed and drawing back the curtains.

Haley held her breath, wondering how she was going to explain the stranger lying asleep.

"Sweet princess," Estelle whispered, as she sat on the edge of the bed.

Haley gave Henry a surprised look.

"You know her?" she asked.

"We met years ago," Estelle answered. "I became the housekeeper of this estate ten years after Zeb Bonner and his family disappeared. I have been here since. Time for my species does not run the same as humans, even while in your world."

Haley's mouth dropped open.

"I have been here for many, many years," Estelle continued. "I have watched new owners come and go; from the time the rift tore our worlds apart."

"You're a fairy?" Henry stammered.

"No, I'm a witch."

"A witch?" the twins responded together.

"Yes, I chose to stay behind after the rift while my family went to the other side."

Haley was stunned. "I had a feeling about you. Why didn't you say anything? Why didn't you tell us?" she asked.

"Would you have believed me? No, you had to find out for yourselves the truth of it," Estelle answered.

"So, you've known about Roan, the palace, and everything?" Haley asked, annoyed.

"Yes. I have been there from time to time throughout the years, visiting, keeping in touch. I've known the prince and princess of Roan and Queen Lilia for a very long time. My family lives in Roan."

Haley was astounded. A million thoughts ran through her mind. "You know Valian?" she asked.

"Quite well," Estelle answered cheerfully.

"Your family lives in Roan?" Henry asked.

"The outskirts actually, my sister Hilda took you in for the night when you first arrived in the outskirts."

"Hilda is your sister?" the twins echoed.

"Yes," Estelle chuckled. "I love my sister and love being a witch, but I chose to stay behind because I love the humans. I am delighted by the way you all act, so free, so ready to accept the challenges of life. Somehow you are equipped with the tools and knowledge to overcome boundaries and face things head on. I am always impressed and fascinated but not surprised. Witches have the same abilities but do not often use them. We rely too much on magic."

Haley sat drinking in every word as Estelle continued.

"When you and your family moved onto the estate, I knew immediately that *you . . .*" she said, looking at Haley, "would be the key to everything. That is when I knew I made the right choice in staying behind."

"How long have you known Sersha was here?" Haley asked.

"Since she arrived, however, I did not wish for her to know I was here. I knew she not only needed to rest, but also to experience human behavior on *this side.*"

They sat quietly for several minutes.

"Do you know why the portals are closed?" Haley asked.

"No, but my postern is working just fine," Estelle answered.

"What? You knew that Sersha was stuck here? Valian has been injured; no telling how badly, and you haven't said a word about having a postern?" Haley demanded. She remembered learning that witches had posterns instead of portals to get from place to place without having to fly.

"Calm down," Estelle said, quietly. "I'm sorry I didn't say anything, but you have to understand that Sersha needed a little time."

"Time for what?" Haley demanded.

Henry looked at his sister in shock at the sarcasm in her voice.

"As I already said, time to heal and time with you, without any influences from the other side."

"I'm not following you," Haley responded impatiently tapping her foot. Estelle sighed.

"Sersha needed time to think things out and listen to others' opinions and ideas, mainly yours. To help her see things differently than what she is used to. By doing that, hopefully she is learning how humans think. It may help her to face what lies ahead and to make the right choices."

Haley sat thinking quietly for a few minutes. "Yes, perhaps you're right," she said softly. "You said your postern is working. Can we get through?"

"Yes. Fairies and witches can get through without assistance but humans can only get through if they are physically touching us. We just need to hold hands as we pass."

"Well, let's go!" Haley exclaimed, suddenly charged, startling them.

"I think we should wait until Sersha wakes up, don't you?" Estelle asked smiling.

Haley rolled her eyes and smiled back, feeling a little guilty for her previous anger toward such a kind woman.

They reminisced about what happened after the twins went to Roan while they waited, they shared about their scary neighbor across the valley, Ike Sr., who they were sure wanted to steal their map. They spoke of their efforts in Roan to save Sarah, Zeb, and their two little daughters,

Susan and Rosie. Haley told about when they met Valian at the old pub in the outskirts.

It began to grow darker outside. Thunder rumbled in the distance.

Shivering, Haley walked over and closed the window.

The clouds hung low and the rain spatter against the glass made it hard to see through.

As she started to turn around, something caught her eye. Opening the window back up, she gazed out at the valley below.

"There's something out there," she whispered.

Henry and Estelle walked over to the window.

"I thought I saw something," she said, squinting.

She scanned the valley floor. Out of the corner of her eye she saw movement. Her eyes fixed on the spot; she stared and then saw it. One of the willow trees seemed to have moved closer toward the estate.

"There, can you see it?" she pointed.

"No," Henry answered.

"It's from the *other side,*" said Estelle quietly, taking a step back. "We have to protect the princess."

"What is it?" Henry asked. "I still can't see it."

"Look. The willow tree. It's getting closer," said Haley, becoming uneasy.

"You have to do something!" said Estelle with urgency in her voice as she walked back to the bed. "We have to protect the princess," she repeated. "No one can know she is here. You will have to go down there."

The twins exchanged worried looks.

"Come on," Henry said, stepping up onto the window ledge. "Estelle is right. We can't let anything happen to Sersha."

Henry's bravery encouraged her and she nodded her head as he jumped. She watched his wings become visible, spreading wide as he sailed through the air.

Climbing onto the ledge, Haley jumped after him.

At the bottom of the bluff, they moved slowly on foot, their eyes fixed on the willow which was only about twenty-five yards away.

Suddenly, a mournful wail broke the silence, making the hair on Haley's arms stand on end. The twins stood rooted to the spot as the willow slowly moved forward. It stopped ten yards away and let out another long, mournful wail.

"Stop it! Haley shouted. Who are you and what do you want?"

The willow bent forward as if bowing.

"I am sorry," said a mournful, ghostly voice. "I did not wish to scare you. I am here seeking Haley and Henry Miles."

"What do you want with them?" Henry asked.

"They are needed back in Roan. I have come to find them."

It let out another wail, giving the twins goosebumps.

"How did you get through?" Haley asked. "The portals are sealed."

The willow gave a shudder.

"Some are working intermittently. They have not been able to fix the problem entirely yet, but the portal in Heime's swamp is still working. I don't know how, but hers never sealed."

"Did you say Heime's swamp?" Haley asked suspiciously.

The willow nodded.

"Heime wouldn't, by chance, be a swamp hag, would she?" Haley asked, remembering the horrible creature she, Valian, Henry, and Sersha had to fight after they used Roan's sacred sphere to travel back in time to save Zeb's wife and girls from being devoured by a swamp hag after they disappeared in the Kootenai River.

"Yes, she is my sister. Do you know her?"

"No, I don't know her and I don't wish to know her. What is your name?" Haley demanded.

"I am Ruena and I don't blame you for not wanting to know her. She and I once lived in the palace, but Heime wasn't satisfied with her position and wanted more power. She tried to deceive the queen but got caught. Since I was with her at the time, the queen thought I was in on it and banished both of us. We lost our home, position, and beauty. Our wings were clipped and we were exiled. I was cursed to live out my life as a willow while Heime was sent to the swamp."

The twins exchanged glances.

"So you are here to help?" Haley asked.

"Yes. I can get them back through the portal in Heime's swamp and help them find Princess Sersha, who has disappeared."

"Where is this portal?" Henry asked.

"Down at the river. It's just a short distance from here, but it's under water, I'm afraid."

A sudden realization dawned on Haley's face. She looked at Henry and saw that he had figured it out as well.

"That's where Sarah and the girls went through," Henry exclaimed. "I don't know why I didn't think of it before!"

Haley turned to Ruena.

"I am Haley, and this is my brother, Henry."

Ruena let out another wail and shook her long willow branches.

"Do you have to do that?" Haley asked. "It's unnerving."

"So, you are the one who has been wailing in this valley all these years," said Henry. "Do you know the people who live here think you are the ghost of Zeb Bonner who disappeared long ago?"

Haley gasped.

Henry quickly turned toward her.

"What?"

"I'll bet you a million dollars the people that have disappeared from Bonners Ferry throughout the years, ended up with the swamp hag. You know Sersha told me the hag eats human flesh."

"Yes," Ruena responded. "She is a sick creature. She is so far gone, there is no hope she will ever change. I don't know how she lives with herself."

"What do you eat?" Henry asked, raising an eyebrow.

"Worms."

"Worms?" said Haley, wrinkling her nose.

"Yes. Worms, grubs, dead and decaying leaves, anything that falls on the ground," Ruena replied.

"Yuck," said Henry in disgust.

"At least I don't eat human flesh."

"I'll give you that one," Henry replied with a grin.

"Well thank you for all your information," said Haley, "but we won't need your assistance with the portal. We will find another way back which doesn't require going into the river. But if you really want to help, you can meet us on the other side when we arrive."

"Oh yes, I would love to help. I'd be honored," said Ruena, bowing again. "When will you arrive?"

"We will meet up when the time is right, probably somewhere in the outskirts and if you are true to your word, perhaps I can get the queen to change her mind about you," said Haley.

"Oh, would you? I would be ever so grateful," Ruena sighed letting out a long wail that sent shivers down Haley's spine.

Haley smiled.

"No problem, but you're going to have to work on that wretched noise."

Ruena bowed again and slowly turned back toward the river.

The twins were excited and took flight back to the west tower. They found Estelle waiting impatiently with towels at the window.

Sersha was awake, pacing the floor. The look of relief she gave Haley as they stepped through the window warmed Haley's heart. She gave Sersha a hug and then the twins quickly told them everything Ruena said as they dried off.

"I think it was wise of you to have your suspicions," said Estelle. "It could have been a trick to get you through the portal, right into the swamp hag's clutches. Good thinking."

"Thanks," said Haley, looking over at the princess.

Sersha looked pale and it worried her.

"You feeling alright?" she asked.

"Sure," Sersha answered. "I'm just a little excited about going home."

"You look pale."

"Yes she does," said Estelle, putting her hand on Sersha's forehead. "You're warm. She has been here too long," she said, turning to Haley. "We need to get her to the other side as soon as possible, like right now."

"What about our parents?" Haley asked.

"I'll put a spell on them like I did the last time you two went to Roan. They'll never even miss us," Estelle replied, waving her hand. "That'll hold them. Their memories of you are gone for now."

They walked down the tower stairs as quietly as they could and headed for Estelle's room just off the grand staircase. Once inside, Haley spotted the postern immediately. It was a huge floor to ceiling painting of a stormy day in a cozy little hollow, with an old waterwheel surrounded by young trees.

"I know this place!" she said, excitedly. "This is next door to Mathilda's food court in the outskirts where we drank rainbow dew with Valian that second day we were there, remember?"

"Oh yeah," Henry grinned.

Estelle smiled and nodded. She took Sersha by the hand and turned to the others.

"Is everybody ready?"

Everyone nodded.

"Wait," she said, grabbing two umbrellas. "It's raining pretty hard."

"How do you know?" Haley asked.

"Look at my postern."

"You mean your postern shows you the current weather in fairy world?"

"Absolutely. Tomorrow my postern will probably look sunny, bright, and warm."

The twins shook their heads in wonder.

"Okay, let's go," said Estelle.

Haley grabbed Sersha's hand and took Henry's hand. Following Estelle's lead, they entered the painting.

Chapter Two

RETURN TO ROAN

As the group stepped through the postern, they were immediately slammed by a driving rain. The wind was blowing so hard it almost knocked them over.

Quickly moving up the street, they pushed against the storm until finally arriving at Hilda's familiar brick cottage.

Estelle grasped the gargoyle knocker and gave it a sharp rap. A few moments later, Hilda opened the door.

"Estelle!" she cried as they embraced. "Merlin's beard, get inside before you catch your death. Haley! Henry! What a surprise!" Then her eyes fell upon Sersha. "Blessed be, come in, child, quickly!" she urged, pulling Sersha through the door.

Hilda ushered everyone into the kitchen. Once she had them seated, she waved her hand, and four towels appeared out of thin air, and they began to dry off. She turned to Sersha.

"Heavens to Betsy, you are white as a ghost. Are you ill, my dear?"

"Actually, I am feeling a little better already," Sersha replied.

"I've got just the thing to perk you up," said Hilda, as she rummaged through the fridge.

She came back with a large cauldron bubbling with hot soup. Bowls and spoons came out of the cupboards by themselves, ready to serve.

"Umm, midnight mushroom?" Sersha asked.

Hilda gave her a wink.

Everyone dove right in as she came back to the table with three steaming mugs filled to the brim with an ember potion.

"Don't drink this until you are ready for bed," she instructed. "It'll make you sleepy."

They ate in silence.

"Dishes, clean yourselves," said Hilda, clapping her hands when they were finished. "Let's go sit by the fire, everyone."

They took their ember potions and retired to the living area, taking seats on the big puffy pillows and cushions in front of the fireplace.

Hilda asked how Sersha ended up on the other side and couldn't get back. Haley and Henry took turns relating how Ruena showed up and retold her story.

"Ruena was always such a kind fairy," said Hilda. "I was totally shocked about what happened with her and Heime. I couldn't believe it."

"Valian . . ." Haley began. "How is he?"

"He's mending, dear," Hilda answered. "He was badly hurt and many didn't think he would survive, but oddly enough, a resident human claimed he had been a doctor when he lived on the other side. All our spells and magic just weren't enough. Luckily, the doctor stopped the bleeding and knew just the right kind of herbs to use. He sewed up Valian's wound, and he began to heal. He is still in the infirmary, hopefully for only a few more days. They say he should be as good as new."

Haley breathed a sigh of relief. Her eyes were starting to get heavy.

"Does anyone know why he couldn't heal himself?" she yawned.

"No, nobody is sure of anything at this point," Hilda answered. "He was very upset that Sersha did not return, and that didn't help his recovery any. He will be so relieved to hear you are all back safe and sound."

"Come on, everyone; let's get you all to bed. We can talk about this in the morning," said Estelle.

Hilda and Estelle ushered them up the stairs toward the bedrooms.

"So, Valian is going to be fine?" Haley murmured as they neared the top step.

"Rest assured," Hilda answered. "He has the best of care. His nurse, Violet, has tended to his every need. She has been with him since he was flown in and hasn't left his side. He has really counted on her company and bedside manner to see him through the toughest part. He is responding well."

Haley frowned as Estelle directed her into her room. As she fell against the pillow, Valian's handsome face and pale blue eyes passed through her mind. She smiled contentedly as she drifted off to sleep, but in the smallest recesses of her mind, an uneasy feeling lurked. It was ever so small, ever so quiet.

After putting their charges to bed, Hilda and Estelle went back to the living area where they sat and enjoyed a snifter of brandy.

"What's with this storm?" Estelle asked. "I've never seen it like this before."

"I know," Hilda replied. "Something's brewing."

Estelle nodded in agreement.

The wind howled outside as the sisters sat watching the flame fairies in the fireplace leap in the air as they danced long into the night.

Haley opened her eyes. It took a moment for her surroundings to register. The air was fresh as a breeze drifting through the open window. Birds were singing their usual chorus.

Sitting up, she looked out the window. The trees were dripping from the rain, and everything looked clean, new, and bright.

She leapt out of bed and went over to the window, taking in a deep breath. It smelled so good. She felt so much more alive here.

After a quick shower, she dressed and bounded down the stairs. She was going to get to see Valian today.

She walked down the hall and stood in the kitchen doorway.

Hilda and Estelle were humming as they busied themselves with breakfast. Haley smiled. They looked content, these two sister witches. It amazed her that she hadn't put two and two together before.

She watched them point to the fridge and stove, ordering various ingredients to appear. As the spices flew from all different directions, she wondered how they kept it all straight.

Hilda turned, grabbing an egg from mid-air, and saw her standing there.

"Mornin' love," she said. "You look like the cat that ate the canary. What are you thinkin' about?"

Estelle turned to look.

"Oh, nothing," Haley answered, walking into the kitchen.

The sisters each gave her a peck on the cheek.

"Where is everybody?" Haley asked.

"Henry is still sleeping," Hilda answered. "I guess the ember potion hit him harder than we anticipated. Sersha went to the infirmary about an hour ago."

"She left without me?" Haley asked, her heart sinking.

"Don't feel bad, my dear," said Hilda. "She just couldn't wait. All she did was pace the floor after she got up. You must realize she and Valian have never been apart, not like this. Besides, the queen had been expecting to see her last night and wasn't happy when she didn't show up."

"I understand," said Haley. "I should have realized how much of a toll it was on her."

"That's all right, dear. You have some breakfast and you can go see him yourself," said Hilda as she loaded a pan with bacon.

"Anything I can do?" Haley asked.

"Not at all," Estelle answered. "You just make yourself comfortable, and we'll call you when breakfast is ready."

Haley walked into the living area and looked around the room. She hadn't really paid a whole lot of attention to what was in this room until now.

Hilda's décor was fascinating. There were all sorts of paintings, mostly of picturesque little hollows and meadows. A tall vase stood in the corner of the room containing several brooms, and she wondered if Hilda flew on any of them.

A portrait of a young couple hung above the fireplace. It drew her attention. She gazed at it. The faces were strangely familiar, but she couldn't think of where she may have seen them before.

The woman had long, beautiful, golden-blond hair and striking green eyes. The man beside her had chestnut hair pulled into a ponytail and sported a firm, square jaw. She stared at him. He looked happy and content, yet there was something about him. She felt connected somehow and could not look away.

The smell of bacon cooking brought Henry downstairs.

"Man, I'm starved," he said as he walked into the kitchen.

"Breakfast is ready, Haley," Estelle called.

Henry sat at the table and began filling his plate with bacon, eggs, fried potatoes, and toast.

After a few minutes, Estelle called again.

"Haley, come and eat."

When she got no response, Hilda went into the living area.

Haley stood in front of the fireplace, looking up at the portrait.

"That's Norman and Mable. Good friends of mine," said Hilda.

"Are they human?" Haley asked.

"Yes. We found them wandering the border of the Woodland realm. When questioned, we found they must have been through such a terrible experience because they had no memory of what had happened to them. They didn't know where they came from or where they were. Obviously, from the other side, but they didn't have a clue. I took them in for a time until they were stable enough to be on their own. Then about twenty years ago or so, I was out hunting a rare toadstool that only grows on the Spicewood realm border. I had foolishly laid my broom against a tree while crawling on my hands and knees, when a wild bulwark attacked me."

"Wow," said Haley, remembering the first time she saw the eight-to-ten-foot-tall guard flowers called bulwarks at Bella's Blossom Shop in Roan. It was a plant with large orange and purple heads that ate just about anything and some varieties could walk. They were designed specifically for protection.

"Thankfully and amazingly," Hilda continued, "Norman came out of nowhere with a machete and cut its stalk in two just as it was about to take my head in its mouth. I still have a scar," she pointed to a jagged scar on the side of her neck. "Norman saved my life."

Haley shook her head in wonder. "He looks familiar to me," she said looking up at the portrait, "like I've seen him before."

"Well, you couldn't have, could you," asked Hilda. "You weren't even born yet. Come. Let's have some breakfast," she said, putting her arm around Haley's shoulders.

"What was their last name?" Haley asked.

"I don't know. They live only about six blocks from here. You could ask them sometime."

Haley was deep in thought all during breakfast.

"Why are you so quiet?" Henry asked.

"Nothing," she answered. "Just wondering when Sersha will be back."

"She probably won't be back for some time," said Hilda. "She still has to go and see the queen after she is finished visiting Valian."

"Well, I'm not going to wait any longer," Haley said impatiently, getting up from the table.

"Wait a few minutes, and I'll go with you," said Henry, taking the last few bites of his eggs.

Haley gave Hilda a hug.

"I hate to eat and fly," she apologized.

"Don't you worry about it," Hilda said, pinching Haley's cheek. "You go and fly safe."

Haley gave Estelle a kiss on the cheek and headed for the door. Henry was right behind her, a piece of toast in his teeth.

They took off heading toward the palace. As they neared the border of Roan, with a snap of spark, they shrank to about the size of a hummingbird. The dwindle drops Valian had given them at Mathilda's were still working.

Henry and Haley flew at tree top level, weaving in and out of the highest branches until finally they could see the palace. It was just as beautiful as Haley remembered, sparkling in the morning sun.

"Should we go see the queen first or go to the infirmary?" Henry yelled.

"Infirmary!" she yelled back without hesitation.

Veering toward the far side of the palace, they crossed over the terraces to a building marked "Infirmary" above the door.

As they landed, Haley remembered the last time they had been there. It was to see Zeb after his rescue from the Cimmerian realm and Molock's clutches.

As they entered, a very energetic fairy gave them the room number for the prince, and they headed that way.

It felt like they were walking in slow motion, and Haley hurried along as if he would be gone before she could get there. She took a deep breath as she pushed open the door to his room.

There he lay, that handsome, golden-haired fairy. Her heart just melted, and she felt weak in the knees. He was asleep, with a slight smile on his lips.

It took a moment for her to realize there was someone else in the room. It was a beautiful fairy with long, golden locks. She looked up as Haley entered the room. Her eyes were a cold, deep purple.

Haley was surprised as her eyes moved over the scene. This fairy was holding Valian's hand!

Her heart began beating a little faster as her breath quickened.

The fairy let go of the prince's hand as she stood and gave Haley a sweet but seemingly insincere smile.

"Good morning. I am Valian's nurse, Violet," she said, holding her hand out as she approached.

Haley politely shook it, finding it as cold as her eyes.

"Valian really can't see visitors right now," she said, walking back to his bed. "He's had a trying morning already, as his sister came to see him earlier. I am afraid she just drained him. Perhaps you could come back later. Maybe he will be up to seeing human visitors then."

That last comment struck a nerve, and Haley struggled to keep her composure.

"All . . . alright. We will be back later," she said, putting emphasis on the will part.

As they were leaving, Haley glanced back to see Violet sitting next to his bed and picking up his hand with a haughty smile on her face.

"Who does she think she is telling me I can't visit?" Haley was saying, as they exited the infirmary.

"I've got just as much right to see him as anyone. I'm closer to him than she will ever be!" she snorted, kicking the air.

"That snotty little fairy, I could just . . . "

"You sound like you're jealous," Henry interrupted, amused.

"Jealous? Jealous of what? That puny little excuse for a fairy? Valian couldn't possibly fall for a plain Jane like her! She's a child!"

Deep down, she knew every word was wishful thinking. Violet was gorgeous, and Haley felt she didn't stand a chance competing for Valian's affection. Violet was young and beautiful; with powers she would never have. She felt totally depressed.

"Come on Hale," said Henry. "Cheer up. Valian knows you care for him and you know he cares for you."

She smiled. "You haven't called me 'Hale' in ages, and you're right. I'm something she will never be, intriguing."

In the back of her mind, she hadn't convinced herself.

They took flight, heading for the palace. It would be good to see the queen again. It was good to be back.

They flew the short distance to the palace courtyard.

Fairies milled about, having brunch and chatting. When the twins landed, there were gasps and cheers. Everyone gathered around them, clapping them on their backs, and hugs of welcome were abundant. Haley smiled shyly while Henry grinned from ear to ear.

"The queen has been expecting you," said one of the older male guardians. "You probably don't remember me, I am Colossus," he said, continuously shaking Haley's hand. "We are so happy to see you've returned. I'll announce you at once," he said, disappearing through one of the large archways.

A few minutes later the sound of a lone trumpet announced the queen's approach. The crowd parted as Queen Lilia stepped through the dozens of fairies.

She was as beautiful as ever in a lavender gown with a crown of diamonds sparkling in her auburn hair. Her radiant face warmed Haley's heart, and they embraced like long-lost friends.

"Welcome back, Haley, Henry. I am so grateful to you both for watching over Sersha. Please, come inside, and we'll talk a bit."

They followed her into the palace, to the familiar room with the plush crimson carpet and blue sofas.

They made themselves comfortable as Reed, the brownie butler, came in with refreshments. He was stealing glances at Haley in such a way it made her uncomfortable, and then he quickly disappeared through a side door.

Everyone began talking at once.

The twins told the queen all about being stuck on the other side, the sealed portals, and discovering Estelle was Hilda's sister.

Haley finally asked. "What about Valian? What is happening with him?"

The concern in her voice confirmed the queen's suspicions.

"You do care for him," she stated.

"Yes, I do," Haley replied.

"That pleases me," said Queen Lilia, smiling warmly.

Haley blushed.

"How is he, really?" she asked anxiously.

"He is doing much, much better," the queen answered. "For a while there, I was afraid . . . "

 She didn't finish.

"Any clues as to why he wasn't mending on his own?" Haley asked.

"None, I have had the best in the infirmary working on it, but no one has any ideas. It's . . . "

Again, she couldn't finish her sentence.

"Anyway, since the day he was brought back from battle, he has had the very best of care. The infirmary staff has been instrumental, and he has an outstanding nurse."

Immediately a vision of Violet holding Valian's hand changed Haley's mood entirely.

Henry, who had been sitting quietly eating cakes and pastries, gave her a bemused look.

She returned the look, and she knew that he knew exactly what she was thinking.

He rolled his eyes and looked away with a grin.

Lilia looked at them both curiously. "Am I missing something?"

"No, I'm just a little stressed about Valian," Haley answered.

"Don't worry; he will be his charming old self in no time."

"That's what worries me," Haley whispered under her breath.

"Well, everyone is back safe and sound," said the queen. "Things have been pretty quiet around here. Have you two made any decision about joining the guardians?"

The invitation to join the guardians was presented to Haley and Henry during the great celebration after they had rescued Zeb from Molock's grasp.

"Sure! When do we start?" Henry responded excitedly.

Haley gave him a surprised look.

"We haven't . . . really talked about it," said Haley, still looking at her brother.

The queen stood and walked over to the window.

"The reason I ask is that there is a secret meeting tonight. Perhaps you would like to join us and see what it's all about."

"A secret meeting?" Henry asked anxiously on the edge of his seat.

"Actually, it was requested by the witches' council. They haven't revealed much about the meeting except to say they have made a discovery concerning Molock and invited just a few of us to sit in."

Haley found witches fascinating. She met some of the witches during the celebration. She was interested in one witch in particular named Tilly. Tilly fit the classic stereotype: the long, dark hair, the pointed hat, and the black cat. Haley was enthralled.

"Sure, we'll check it out," she answered excitedly.

Just then the door opened. Sersha came in, all smiles and looking one hundred percent better.

"You look great," said Haley, giving her a big hug.

Lilia gave her daughter a kiss on the cheek.

"Henry and Haley will be joining us tonight," said the queen with great satisfaction.

"Wonderful!" Sersha exclaimed, pleased.

"Will Valian be there?" Haley asked hopefully.

"No, I'm afraid not," said Sersha. "Don't worry, he's in good hands."

Haley sighed heavily and shook her head.

Lilia and Sersha looked at each other questioningly but didn't respond.

"Speaking of my dear brother, I'll bet you'd like to go see him now, yes?"

"Actually, we've already been to the infirmary, but the nurse told us he couldn't have visitors because he had already had a *trying morning,"* said Haley, mockingly.

"Well, thank goodness he has such a caring staff to take care of him," said Lilia.

Haley pondered whether she should bring it up and decided to throw caution to the wind. Even so, Violet was a fairy, and she realized she should proceed tactfully.

"What do you think of his nurse?" she asked casually.

"Violet? She is wonderful. She has given Valian one hundred ten percent of her time and is devoted to seeing him recover," Lilia answered.

"Yes, I could see that," Haley responded, with a hint of sarcasm that Lilia and Sersha didn't detect, but Henry, on the other hand, raised an eyebrow as he listened to the conversation.

"I don't know," Haley continued. "Something about her doesn't seem right."

"What do you mean?" Lilia asked, concerned.

"I'm not sure," she responded nonchalantly. "I can't quite put my finger on it." She paused for a moment then just blurted it out. "There's something false about her, and I don't trust her."

"I don't understand," uttered the queen, alarmed.

Henry looked at Sersha, then the queen, and back at Haley.

"Haley is just concerned about his recovery and wants the best possible care for him. It's not easy to trust someone you don't know. That's all," said Henry.

Haley looked at her brother gratefully. She could see she was about to step out of bounds. After all, they weren't guardians yet. Who would believe her suspicions without proof?

"Yes, that's it," Haley said quickly.

The queen and Sersha seemed satisfied with Henry's explanation.

"Shall we have some lunch?" Sersha asked, walking toward the door.

"I'm famished," Henry agreed.

They had lunch out in the courtyard and enjoyed the warmth of the sun and fresh air. Haley decided to put her suspicions about Violet aside and just focus on being back in Roan.

Chapter Three

THE SECRET MEETING

The twins enjoyed a quiet afternoon with Sersha. They took a sail through the city, checking out all the quaint shops tucked away among the trees. Things had changed substantially in the short time the twins had been gone. Haley commented how some of the shops seemed to have disappeared.

Sersha explained that fairies relocated regularly to keep potential enemies from knowing where anyone was. Haley had hoped to stop at Bella's Blossom Shop and was disappointed that it wasn't there, however she was still thrilled at how beautiful this place was.

Sunbeams danced in the trees, highlighting the tons of flowers that grew everywhere. It was a relaxing afternoon.

They spent the last hour before dinner resting on the banks of a mermaid pool.

Mermaids were exquisite. Their scales shone in the sun like millions of colorful mirrors. Several basked in the sun on the large boulders that stuck out of the water. They all had long hair which they combed for hours.

Henry kept quiet the entire time, and Haley noticed a strange look in his eyes as he gazed at the mermaids intently. He had a hint of a smile on his face, and she wondered if he was finally becoming interested in girls. She had always heard that girls matured sooner than boys did. She found the moment rather amusing. He had always teased her about being boy crazy, now it looked as if the tables were turning. He let out a satisfied sigh, and she smiled to herself.

As the sun began to set, one by one the mermaids slipped into the water and with a splash of their tails and disappeared into the depths.

"We'd better be getting back. You know how my mother is about being late," said Sersha. "Besides we need time to get ready for the meeting."

Enjoying such a pleasant afternoon, Haley had forgotten about the meeting. All the stories about witches she had heard while growing up were fun and mysterious, and she couldn't wait to get there.

She began asking Sersha all sorts of questions as they flew back to the palace.

"How long have witches been here? Do they really practice magic and spells? How well do you know Tilly?"

"Well," Sersha began, "they have been here from the beginning, I suppose. I believe after the rift they kept to themselves and stayed within their own realm, but through the years they have become somewhat of an ally and venture out to attend some of our gatherings. Still, they are elusive and never give out more information than they see necessary. As for Tilly, she is old and wise, very mysterious, and I suspect is in a high position with the council, but who knows?"

Haley pondered all this information in silence.

They zipped through the branches of the giant trees. The sun was almost set and the sparkling castle slowly began to lose its luster.

A layer of fog began to creep in. Hazy, twinkling lights began to appear in the tiny houses nestled in the trees. Plumes of smoke wafted from chimneys, and the aroma reminded Haley of her own world and her first visit to the Owens Country store in Bonners Ferry on that chilly, stormy day. The day she and her mother heard about the legend of Bonners Ferry, where Zeb Bonner lost his wife and children, drowned in the Kootenai River, and how he was never heard from again, about other people disappearing through the years, some going mad. It seemed so long ago, even though it happened only weeks ago.

They landed in the courtyard and went in to dinner. The palace dining room was almost empty. Only the guardians attended this evening, and they rose from their seats and bowed as the trio entered.

Sersha and the twins sat down and listened to the light conversation as they waited for Queen Lilia to arrive.

After several minutes, the familiar gong sounded as she was carefully escorted inside.

Side doors opened, and the brownie servants entered with trays steaming with all sorts of delights.

Halfway through dinner an orderly from the infirmary came bursting into the room, panting and out of breath.

Several male guardians rose quickly, angered at the intrusion of the private dinner. As they approached the orderly, the queen raised her hand.

"Wait; let us hear what he has to say."

"Pardon, pardon, your majesty," the fairy apologized quickly.

"What is the meaning of this intrusion?" one of the guardians demanded.

"Prince Valian . . ."

"What about the prince?" Lilia whispered.

"He is completely healed!"

Everyone looked at each other in surprise.

"We don't know how or why," he continued excitedly. "He just got right out of bed and demanded for us to release him. We examined him and his wound has all but disappeared. We questioned his nurse, but she is at a loss as well. He said he was starving and as soon as he was dressed, would be coming back to the palace."

The dining room erupted in cheers, clapping, and laughter. Lilia sat down with a sigh of relief. One of the guardians clapped the orderly on the back and dismissed him to return to the infirmary.

Haley's heart began to beat faster at the thought of seeing Valian, strong and handsome and back to his old self again.

A few minutes later, the orderly escorted the prince into the dining hall.

He was handsome indeed and seemed even more muscular and alive.

Haley's breathing increased with each step as he approached the group.

As he neared the table and embraced his mother, Haley knew she had fallen in love with him. Her heart was doing flip-flops and she had butterflies in her stomach.

He looked at each guardian with compassion and gratefulness, and when his eyes met hers, her heart seemed to melt and her knees began to shake. She thought she would faint dead away when he smiled. Just as he was about to speak, a beautiful blonde with striking violet eyes, stepped out from behind him.

Haley was jerked out of her dreamy state as if she had been slapped in the face. Although her heart was still pounding madly, now it was for a different reason.

As the rivals looked at each other, something happened that no one else could see. It seemed there was an understanding between them. They were enemies.

Haley trembled as Valian kissed her hand.

"Milady, it warms my heart to see you again," he said, turning toward his chair.

His abrupt move confused her. She glanced at Violet, who had a haughty sneer on her face.

Valian held out his hand toward Violet, and as she took it, she shot Haley a defiant look.

"You all know my nurse Violet," Valian began as he directed her to the seat beside his own. "Everyone insisted she accompany me as a condition of my release, to be sure I have continuous care until they are satisfied that I am completely well."

"I agree," said the queen, with a warm smile. "I don't have the answer for your speedy recovery, but I am pleased that you have Violet at your side."

Haley's heart sank. She felt defeated. Everyone seemed to think that Violet was the answer to their worries, but she knew something wasn't right, and she wasn't going to give up as easily as Violet might think.

She ate her dinner in silence as everyone around her chatted and enjoyed each other's company.

They gathered in a smaller chamber after dinner to discuss the upcoming meeting.

As everyone got comfortable, Reed entered with some after-dinner refreshments and, as usual, gave her a strange look as he passed. She was beginning to sense that Roan's occupants were not all the innocent, helpless beings she was led to believe they were or something had happened to change things.

Through all that had transpired so far this evening, Haley was still excited about meeting with the witches and was glad Valian would be going along, even though he had to have that crummy nurse with him.

Everyone went to change into the appropriate clothing for the trip and rejoined in the courtyard.

By now, the fog was so thick that you could cut it with a knife. It was going to be difficult to navigate, so everyone paired up. Valian and Violet were together, much to Haley's disappointment.

They flew for just over an hour and landed on the edge of a large glade blanketed in night mists. Several old cottages built of stone were hidden in the trees, completely covered in moss and ivy.

Haley had a hard time focusing on anything. The torches made a feeble attempt to light the area, casting small, dull beams around them. Thin plumes of smoke rose slowly from the chimneys, mingling with the fog.

The doorway to one of the cottages was illuminated by a fire inside.

A hooded figure appeared out of the surrounding darkness and escorted them toward the cottage, where a young witch stood waiting.

She had pitch-black hair, eyes, and the whitest skin Haley had ever seen. She doubted the witch had ever seen daylight.

"Come," she said, leading them inside.

As usual, the outside of the building was deceiving as the inside was enormous. Dimly lit lanterns led them down a long hallway into a large, smoke-filled room where the smell of incense was strong. Wooden benches lined the walls, with several long tables in the center. Haley marveled at the brooms standing straight up without the assistance of something to lean on.

They were led to one of the tables. As they took their seats, witches began entering the room. Haley could have sworn they were coming through the walls.

Their black hooded robes were lined with bright satin fabrics. Each witch was uniquely different.

When Tilly entered, everyone parted to let her through. She wore a pointed black hat, and her pitch-black hair was so dark and shining it almost looked blue. The inside of her cape matched her emerald, green eyes that immediately spotted Haley seated at the next table. It gave Haley goosebumps. A beautiful black cat sat on her shoulder; its tail curled around her neck like a thin furry muffler. Tilly petted the cat with her long, red nails as she walked past and took her seat at the head table.

The witches found their places and sat silently. It was unnerving. The twins gave each other a look with raised eyebrows. Haley looked at the three empty seats at the head of Tilly's table and wondered who they were waiting for.

Glancing around the table at all the silent witches, she suddenly felt uncomfortable. The urge to get up and run was almost overwhelming. Just as she felt she was about to burst out of her seat, the three spots were filled. She did a double take, wondering where they came from.

Sitting at the head of the table in a black robe was one of the most handsome men she had ever seen. He was just as handsome as Valian. His black hair matched his eyes. His square jaw had just a hint of a smile. The look in his eyes seemed all-knowing, as though they could look into your soul and know just what you were thinking and feeling. He had a deep dark tan, which surprised her. Her impression was that witches only came out after dark.

He was flanked by two other handsome males, both dressed in black robes and deeply tanned. She sensed they were just below him in rank.

He looked around the table, acknowledging each one present, and they in turn nodded their heads. One by one, his eyes met each individual.

The room was so quiet you could have heard a pin drop a mile away. She felt this man was probably one of the most prominent figures in the council.

His eyes found hers, and she held her breath. The look in his eyes was almost intoxicating. He looked at her as if he knew her. She felt their gaze locked together and she was powerless to look away. Haley felt confused. *"Where am I? Why am I here?"* she thought to herself. She tried to think, to remember.

As he looked on to the next witch in attendance, it was as if someone slammed a door, snapping her back to reality.

"Welcome to our guests," he said.

His voice was deep and dark somehow, yet it was soothing at the same time.

Haley's heart skipped a beat.

"And a special welcome to our human guests," he continued, locking eyes with her again.

She felt flushed, and a warm feeling traveled through her in a split second.

"Allow me to introduce myself; I am Maximillion, Prince Sorcerer of the Lesothorian realm . . ." he paused.

"A little history for our guests . . . most of us arrived here from the Mediterranean just after the rift . . ."

As he continued, Haley stopped listening and got lost in his deep voice. She didn't hear a word he said. She was off sitting by a babbling brook, basking in the sun, surrounded by fields of wildflowers and songbirds.

Quite suddenly, it was all over. Everyone was quiet as Maximillion greeted those around him, shaking hands.

She looked over toward Henry. He had a strange look on his face as if to say, "What happened to you?" Everyone stood waiting for the head sorcerer, hoping he would pass by with a word or a touch.

As he approached Haley, again her heart skipped a beat. Looking into his eyes, deep, dark, and mysterious, it made her feel warm and relaxed.

He stopped in front of her and took her hand. His touch was gentle, yet strong. He towered over her by at least a foot and was by far the most muscular man she had ever met.

As he raised her hand to his lips, he looked deep into her eyes, and they spoke to her as if he had whispered into her ear.

"You are mine," they said. "You will be my bride."

She froze. Her heart was pounding, and she felt very weak and lightheaded. There were murmurs from the crowd as she collapsed.

"Haley!" Henry cried out.

Maximillion caught her, scooping her up in his arms as if she were as light as a feather.

Henry and Valian began to rush forward but were blocked by the two male sorcerers.

Violet stood a short distance away with a desperate look on her face as Valian showed his concern.

Queen Lilia took Valian by the arm.

"He is very powerful, I am sure he can help her," she whispered.

Everyone stood back as Maximillion lowered her onto one of the benches along the wall, bent over her, and kissed her.

Henry looked on with his mouth hanging open. He looked over and watched Valian's face turn crimson. His jaw was firmly locked, and his fists were clenched. He made a move to go forward when Sersha intervened.

"What's the matter with you?" she whispered, grabbing his arm and pulling him back into the crowd.

"Haley is mine," he growled.

"What do you mean yours?" she asked, pulling him toward the hall. "You can't insult the sorcerer."

Valian jerked his arm away from her in anger.

Sersha looked stunned and hurt.

Lilia glanced toward them and saw the look on Valian's face. She hurried over and helped Sersha steer him down the hall.

"What is wrong?" Lilia asked.

"Haley is mine," Valian repeated.

"Yours?"

Valian's face was beet red.

The queen looked at him with growing concern. "Are you jealous?"

He didn't answer.

"I've seen this before, but never from a fairy. This is a human emotion," she stated, ushering Valian and Sersha outside.

Violet stood at the window with a look of desperation still on her face, watching Valian as he talked to the queen in low tones. Turning, she glanced back at Maximillion. Her face calmed a bit as she watched him lovingly tending to Haley. A sly smile grew on her face, and she sashayed over toward the sorcerer. His attraction to Haley was clear.

She slinked her way past the other sorcerers who were busy watching Henry and leaned close to Maximillion, whispering in his ear.

"She really is quite lovely . . . isn't she?" she said softly.

Maximillion looked up at her.

"Stunning," he answered.

Violet looked down at Haley with distaste. "There is something about her . . . I think she likes you."

He looked at Violet, puzzled.

"You do like her, don't you?" she asked playfully.

He looked down at Haley.

"I will make you mine," he said under his breath.

"I could help you . . . if you wanted me to. Haley is a good friend of mine. I could influence her if you get my meaning."

"I'm intrigued," Maximillion replied with a devilish grin. "And pray tell, what would be the price for this great favor?" he asked in a deep, dark tone of voice.

Violet took a step back and stuttered nervously. "Ah . . . ah . . . nothing much, a pittance really, a love potion," she whispered.

Maximillion gave her an amused look. "What is a child like you going to do with a love potion?"

Violet looked hurt.

"And who is going to be the lucky recipient of this love potion, should I grant it?" he asked.

He followed Violet's gaze toward Valian standing in the doorway.

"Ah, you wish to become part of the royal family," he said, smirking. She blushed.

"You know love potions can backfire if one is not careful. Are you sure you want to play this game?" he asked.

Violet broke her gaze, looked up at the sorcerer, and nodded.

"Very well, I will bargain with you, but be warned. If you cross me . . . " he trailed off, looking back down at Haley.

Violet slowly backed away with a worried look on her face.

As Violet left the room, Haley opened her eyes.

"What happened?" she asked, a little alarmed at everyone staring at her. She looked up at Maximillion. When their eyes met, she felt a flutter in her stomach.

"It's all right, my dear," he said softly. "You are safe. You fainted."

"My goodness, I'm so embarrassed," she said, getting to her feet.

"There is no need," he said, taking her hand to help her.

She looked around for Henry and the rest of her group.

Henry rushed toward her.

Maximillion raised his hand, and the other sorcerers let him pass.

"Are you alright?" Henry asked, distressed by his sister's collapse.

"I'm fine," Haley answered reassuringly. "Just too much excitement, I guess."

Henry took her arm and led her toward the hall.

"What happened to you?" he whispered. "You looked like you were off in space or something during the meeting."

"What do you mean?" Haley asked.

"Well it was like the light was on but nobody was home. Your eyes were open but you were off in la-la land."

Haley frowned. She tried to think of what happened, but all she could remember was listening to the sorcerer as he began speaking. The rest was just a blur.

"What was the meeting about?" she asked, embarrassed again.

He rolled his eyes at her, and they both giggled. That lightened the mood a bit and Haley began to feel better.

Henry began to explain the meeting as they walked down the hall, just mentioning the highlights.

"Apparently, it was reported that Molock has a new apprentice,; someone to run around and do his dirty work for him. A group of witches spotted him as they left the Cimmerian realm several nights ago. The individual had a lantern and was just about to enter the cave of the dead mountain. He was cloaked so they didn't get a look at his face, but they said they could almost feel the evil emanating from him as they flew by."

Just then Haley saw Valian, Lilia, and Sersha just outside the door. She broke into a big smile and went to greet them.

"Haley!" Valian cried as she approached.

She rushed into his open arms.

"Are you alright?" he asked, holding her at arm's length looking her over for injuries.

"I'm fine, really. You know how fascinated I am about witches. It was just too much excitement, that's all."

"Are you sure?" he asked again, giving her another hug.

"Yes. I am totally fine."

She was beaming. Her heart was warm, and she felt so safe in Valian's arms. She wished she could freeze time.

As they embraced, Maximillion watched from the doorway as Violet looked on from behind one of the nearby trees. Though they weren't near each other, they glanced in each other's direction. Violet had a look of sinister determination and Maximillion, envy and animosity.

As they flew back to the palace, Haley thought about all Henry had told her. A new apprentice. She wondered who it was and how they were going to stop him from whatever Molock had in store.

As she climbed into bed, she couldn't help thinking about Maximillion. He was charming yet so mysterious. Again, she tried to remember what had happened at the meeting. Haley seemed to recall Maximillion telling her that he loved her and wanted to marry her. She shook her head. No, that obviously didn't happen. Still, she couldn't help but feel that something unusual took place between the two of them.

As she drifted off to sleep, Valian and Maximillion played tag with her affections. She smiled, then frowned, and smiled again as sleep took her.

Violet flew back toward the palace with the others to avoid raising suspicion, and as soon as the opportunity presented itself, she veered away like she was heading for home, but was soon headed back to the witches' camp.

She flew through the night mists and arrived back in the Lesothorian realm where Maximillion was waiting.

The fog had cleared, and a fingernail moon shimmered in the night sky like a sharp sickle ready to strike. Crickets were chirping out their night messages, keeping in tune with the hundreds of frogs croaking in the night mists. A soft breeze held the musty scent of the damp forest. It was the kind of night Haley would have appreciated had she ventured out.

Maximillion was hovering on his broom just over the cottage. Violet hovered beside him briefly before he took off like a shot, leading her deep into the forest.

The trees were gigantic and very old. They were packed together so tightly Violet was hit several times by branches blocking her way. It had been centuries since the forest floor had seen any daylight. She flew as closely as she could so she wouldn't lose him.

They arrived at his bungalow. The door was hidden in the base of an extremely large tree, virtually undetectable.

Maximillion snapped his fingers, and the door slowly opened. A fire roared in the fireplace. Wall-mounted lamps lit themselves as he passed by, revealing a magnificent den. There was an entire wall lined with books floor to ceiling, old books, worn and faded.

"I'm impressed," said Violet. "I see you are well educated."

Maximillion didn't reply.

The room was furnished with large leather sofas and chairs. Old portraits of witches long gone hung on the walls. Alarmingly, there were several witches tied to the stake and others that had been hung by the neck.

Maximillion placed his broom alongside the fireplace and sat in one of the thick leather chairs. He lit some incense and poured a smoky liquid from the large flask tied about his waist into a jewel-encrusted stein. He watched Violet with interest as she looked around the room.

"Would you like a drink?" he asked as their eyes met.

"Sure," she answered apprehensively.

He snapped his fingers and a mug appeared in his hand already filled with the same smoky potion.

She took it and sat down in the other chair, which engulfed her. She nervously sipped her drink as she continued to survey the room. Her eyes were drawn back to the portrait of the witches about to be burned at the stake. She looked curious, but the sorcerer gave her no explanation. His silence made her fidget uncomfortably.

"So . . ." he began, startling her. "Are you ready for your love potion?"

"Yes," she answered in an excited whisper.

Her greedy eyes darted around the room, searching for a love potion.

Maximillion drew a small container from inside his cloak. It was a very old brass box, about the size of a book of matches. In it was a small amount of fine, black powder, almost like black, shining sand.

He stared at her for a moment. His black eyes seemed even blacker, and he had just a hint of a smile.

"This potion has immediate effects. It must be mixed with the blood of a black Peruvian toadstool and drunk within one hour. This has to be exact. If you are not precise the consequences . . ." his voice trailed off.

Violet reached for the box with trembling hands. Just as she was about to grab it, he pulled his hand back.

She quickly looked up at him.

"Remember my words," he said, handing her the box.

She snatched it from him like a spoiled child stealing a cookie. As she turned to go, he spoke again.

"By the way, you have to take the potion," he smiled mischievously.

"Huh?"

"The only way the potion will work is if you take it."

"I don't understand. I thought it was to be given to the one you wanted it to work on. I . . . I don't feel comfortable taking the potion myself, I . . ."

"Oh, I'm sorry. If you don't want it," he said, holding out his hand.

"No! No, that's okay. I'm okay with it. I was just nervous for a minute. It'll be fine. I'm good," she babbled on, her voice shaking.

"Are you quite sure?" he asked with that same mischievous smile.

"I'm sure. Thank you."

"Don't forget what I said; you must be precise. I expect you to deliver on your promise upon the harvest moon. It will be a glorious wedding. Every witch will be in attendance and pay homage to me and my bride . . ." he trailed off.

Violet nodded, rolling her eyes as she turned for the door. She paused for a moment as an idea popped into her head, and she turned back toward the sorcerer.

"You know . . . in order for this plan to succeed, she is going to need to see your interest. I can influence her all you want, but you will need to be convincing also."

"I have every intention to do so," he replied sarcastically.

"I'm sorry. I hope I haven't overstepped my bounds. I'm sure you will have no trouble. Good night," she threw over her shoulder as she stepped out the door.

As she flew back toward Roan, she kept her eye open for the Peruvian toadstools he had told her about and found a patch growing on the south side of an old dead tree.

Stashing them inside her cloak, she flew like the wind, delighted by her cunning.

It was nearly two in the morning when she arrived back at her cottage in the crook of a giant elder tree.

It was a quaint little place. The outside was constructed with thick bark. It was sturdy and smelled like old wood. The inside was lavishly decorated with long draping silks hanging in the windows and separating each room.

She promptly went to a small wooden bowl in her kitchenette and retrieved the small box and toadstools from her cloak. She pondered for a moment, trying to remember Maximillion's instructions.

"Now, did he say to take it after one full hour or was it before a full hour?" she asked herself. "I can't remember."

Back at the palace, Queen Lilia was up late, sitting in the library with Valian.

"I don't know what's wrong with me," said Valian, pacing the floor. "I've got this weird feeling I've never felt before. I think I felt . . . anger toward the sorcerer for showing Haley such attention, and when he kissed her, my body got all hot, and I just wanted to strike him. What is happening to me, Mother?" he asked, frustrated.

"I don't know," she answered. "You are displaying a human emotion, but why, I don't understand. Perhaps you left the infirmary too soon."

"I don't think so. I feel fine physically."

"Just the same, let's just have you checked out to make sure. In the meantime, I will do some research to see if I can come up with any ideas. Now you get to bed. You need your rest."

Lilia retired to her room with a very troubled look on her face.

Chapter Four

A DREAM COME TRUE

The next morning Valian was feeling much better. Yesterday's events had faded, and he had a spring in his step as he went to breakfast.

When he arrived in the courtyard, it was already crowded with fairies, eating, chatting, and enjoying a beautiful morning.

Haley had just arrived minutes before and sat at a small table waiting for him. She spotted him as he made his way through the crowd.

He saw her and waved, wearing the biggest smile. It warmed her heart.

"I'm famished," he said, sitting down beside her.

He helped himself to a large serving of flapjacks and ham with a large glass of rainbow dew to wash it down

"I'm just starved," he said, smiling at her.

"You sound just like Henry," she giggled.

They ate in silence, listening to all the fairies. Most talk was light and cheery; however, several were discussing the idea of an apprentice actually joining up with Molock the Merciless.

"What shall we do today?" Valian asked with a satisfied sigh, rubbing his belly.

"I don't know," she answered with a smile.

"Let's go for a sail, just you and me. We'll make it a picnic, what do you say?" he asked with a twinkle in his eye.

"That sounds lovely," she answered, blushing.

Finally, they would have a chance to be alone together. She had been so stressed at the thought of losing him to Violet; she jumped at the chance of having him all to herself.

Valian excused himself to go have lunch packed while she went back to her room to change.

Haley chose the beautiful, backless, peach gown Valian had given her back at Hilda's place. It seemed like such a long time ago that he had given her the elixir so she could grow wings. She smiled at the memory.

As Haley turned in front of the mirror, the sun caught the glint of something shiny on the floor along the base of the wall. She bent down and, with astonishment, picked up Sarah's ruby necklace.

Her excitement faded quickly as she wondered how it got there. Why had no one found it just lying on the floor for everyone to see? She had searched her room a dozen times after she discovered it missing. This was strange and she felt uneasy. Someone must have placed it there on purpose. Perhaps the thief had a guilty conscience.

She shrugged her shoulders and smiled as she admired it. Sarah would be so delighted to get it back. She put the necklace around her neck, and at that moment, she could feel the love Sarah had for Zeb.

Haley suddenly felt as if she had just invaded Sarah's privacy and quickly took it off, slipped it into the deep pocket of her gown and left for the courtyard.

Valian was waiting with a big grin on his face.

Henry had arrived and was busy shoveling in the food.

"How ya doin,' sleepyhead?" Haley asked, messing up his hair.

"Great," he mumbled between mouthfuls, "couldn't be better. Where are you off to?" he asked, eyeing Valian's lunch bag.

"We're off for a sail," Haley answered with a smile.

"I'm almost done with breakfast," he replied.

"It's just the two of us on this one," Valian said quickly. "You can come next time."

Henry looked a little hurt, yet at the same time, he looked like he understood and gave Valian a thumbs up. "Actually, I was thinking of going to visit Zeb and Sarah today . . . " he began.

"Oh! That reminds me," Haley interrupted. "Sorry, Henry," she apologized, "but look what I found this morning!"

She pulled out Sarah's necklace. The brilliant, red stone gleamed.

"You found it!" Henry exclaimed. "Where?"

"It was on the floor in my room. I can't imagine how it got there. I think someone deliberately put it there for me to find."

"That's odd," said Valian, taking the necklace. He examined it but found nothing out of the ordinary. "I'll have to have a word with the cleaning staff."

Haley put the necklace back in her pocket.

"You want me to take it to Sarah?" Henry asked.

"No, I want to give it to her myself. I can't wait to see her face."

"Well? Shall we?" Valian asked, taking Haley's hand.

They fanned their wings and leaped from the balcony.

Henry watched as they sailed over the treetops and disappeared into the canopy. They were like two butterflies floating on the wind.

Haley and Valian flew for several miles, hand in hand, glancing back and forth at each other. Haley would blush, and Valian would smile.

They dodged in and out between the great trees, weaving back and forth, over great forests and across beautiful meadows full of giant black-eyed Susans until Valian called out for a breather.

As they landed atop one of the magnificent black and yellow heads, Haley giggled.

"What?" Valian asked.

"I would never have dreamt I would be sitting on top of a flower, flying everywhere I go . . . with you."

They looked into each other's eyes.

"Neither have I," he said softly.

Haley felt herself drawn to him. Her heart beat faster. She felt like he was about to kiss her.

"Hey! I want to show you something," he said, suddenly, startling her.

"Oh, okay," she replied, slightly confused.

"Come on," he urged, taking her by the hand.

Haley was surprised to find his hand sweaty. *"He's nervous,"* she thought to herself and smiled. *"To think, a strong, handsome fairy like Valian, being nervous."*

As they cleared the black-eyed Susans, she gasped at the sight in front of her.

"Change!" Valian called out.

With the familiar snap of a spark, they changed to normal size and landed in a small grove of trees, sparkling with what Haley thought were red berries. It only took a moment for her to realize they were not berries at all but rubies, thousands of rubies. They tinkled softly as the warm breeze passed through the branches.

"My goodness," she exclaimed. "I've never seen anything so beautiful."

"Neither have I," Valian said, softly, walking toward her.

He took her gently into his arms and when his lips met hers, she melted. Her legs became like putty. She was in heaven.

His kiss lasted but a second, but for Haley it was as if time stood still. As they drew apart, she blushed again.

"Haley, I care for you very deeply," he said, taking her hand.

"I care for you too," she said, trembling slightly.

She was sure he could hear her heart pounding.

Valian looked up at the shining stones hanging in large clumps. He reached up into the branches and plucked a delicate, brilliant ruby and placed it in her hand.

"My heart is yours, milady," he said.

She knew in her heart that Valian was the one for her. She felt as if her heart would explode with joy, she was so happy.

"Oh, Valian, I am so glad you feel this way. When I saw you with Violet . . ." she paused.

"Violet? You thought I cared for Violet?"

"Well, I . . ."

He began to laugh, the kind of deep laugh that comes from the gut.

"Don't laugh!" she said, embarrassed.

"I'm sorry," he continued chuckling, "but Violet? She was my nursemaid, nothing more."

"Well, I think it was something more for Violet."

"I don't know how you could think that."

"Maybe it was the way she was holding your hand at the infirmary and maybe it was because she wouldn't let me visit you."

"What? She wouldn't let you visit?" he asked, sounding upset.

"Yes. She said you had had too much excitement already from Sersha's visit and that maybe you could handle human visitors later."

Valian did not look pleased at this news.

"You have nothing to worry about from her," he said sarcastically.

Haley had never heard this tone of voice from him before.

"You okay?" she asked.

"Excellent!" he answered, scooping her up in his arms and twirling her around.

Haley laughed with delight.

"Come on, let's go have some lunch," he said, grabbing her hand.

They flew to the edge of a beautiful lake and sat on the bank and ate.

Haley dangled her feet in the water, fanning her wings like a butterfly. There was a comfortable silence between them. They watched the clouds float by, picking out imaginary animals in the sky and laughing at the two-headed duck Haley spotted.

Valian suddenly dropped a bombshell.

"I want to marry you Haley."

Her mouth dropped open.

"M . . . marry me?"

She couldn't believe her ears. Was her dream coming true right here and now? She was quiet for a moment.

"Valian . . . I'm flattered. I would love to marry you, but I'm not old enough."

"It wouldn't be right now," he responded. "Manwan's are required to wait three years after getting engaged before they can wed."

"Oh . . . " she sighed, relieved. "I'm not ready for marriage yet but being engaged is different. Besides, my family will need to meet you and . . . boy, how is that going to work? They will never believe it. I can hardly believe it."

"Fear not, my darling," he said tenderly. "All will be well."

They spent the rest of the afternoon talking, walking hand in hand, and flying from one pretty spot to another.

They changed size and sat perched in an aspen above one of the many mermaid pools in the Woodland realm.

Haley marveled at the mermaids' long tails as they sunned themselves and noticed how attentive they were to their surroundings. They didn't miss a thing.

"What do they eat?" she asked.

"Fish," he answered.

"Fish is good," she commented. "It's a better diet than Ruena has."

Valian looked at her, surprised.

"You know Ruena? How do you know her?"

She explained how Ruena showed up on the other side, looking for her and Henry and her offer to help.

"No one is allowed to go through the portals without permission. It is forbidden," he said, concerned.

"It's okay," Haley interjected. "She came to help."

"No," Valian answered, sternly. "Haley, you must be careful. Ruena was banished along with her sister. She is not to be trusted."

"She seemed so sincere," Haley murmured. "You know I had the impression that fairy world was safe and full of kindness and innocence, but it sure doesn't seem to be the case at all," she frowned.

"Sadly, Molock the Merciless has seen to that," Valian replied and spit on the ground.

"Well don't you worry my darling, all will be well. We'll see to that. One way or another we will defeat him," she stated defiantly.

Valian couldn't help but smile at her.

"That's what I love about you. You have such a fiery spirit. You are a natural Guardian."

Haley smiled and sighed happily.

It was getting late, and the couple flew to the outskirts to Mathilda's for a mug of rainbow dew out on the terrace.

"Do you remember when I first brought you here?" Valian beamed.

"Like it was yesterday," she answered. She began to laugh. "Remember when Henry ate his dwindle drop and disappeared? How I shrieked?"

"Yeah, that was a good one," he chuckled.

The familiar brownie with the filthy apron brought them their mugs and shuffled back inside.

"I am going to announce our engagement tonight at dinner," said Valian. "I hope that meets with your approval."

"Yes, of course," Haley beamed. "Won't everyone be surprised?"

As the afternoon wound down, they finished their drinks, and Valian went inside to pay while Haley sat enjoying the view of the dozens of waterfalls below Mathilda's. The creaking of the old waterwheel next door was soothing.

"What a perfect day," she said to herself. Valian really did love her, and she felt like a fool that she ever doubted it. How could she have even considered Violet a threat? It all seemed like a bad dream.

Valian came out of Mathilda's wearing a huge grin. "Come," he said, taking her hand.

He led her around the corner toward the waterwheel, to a bench beneath the young trees.

"I have a gift for you," he said as she sat down.

She looked up at him and smiled.

"What is it?" She asked.

He handed her a long, ruby chain.

She had never seen anything like it.

"What is it exactly?"

"It is a symbol of our betrothal. You will wear it on your right wrist until our wedding day, at which time the ruby I gave you today will be placed in this empty chamber."

"Where did you get this?" she asked, admiring the chain.

"I gathered these rubies after you and Henry went home. I had it made here at Mathilda's. It's quite a simple process really. We have very skilled craftsmen in the land."

He smiled that smile, which made her go weak in the knees again.

"It's beautiful," she whispered. "How do you wear it?"

Valian took the chain and looped it around her wrist several times, around her middle finger and across her hand, fastening it with a gold clasp. It was stunning against her golden tan. She admired it as they flew back to the palace. Valian watched her, pleased with her delight.

Haley was glowing as she walked into her room to freshen up. She showered and changed into a simple lilac-colored gown, backless of course. All female faeries wore backless because of their wings.

She slid into a pair of satin slippers and took another quick look in the mirror as someone knocked on her door.

"Ah, the steward," she thought. *"Right on schedule."* "Come in," she yelled.

The door opened and closed.

"I'll be right there," she called out.

With a final adjustment to her hair, she turned and gasped.

"Violet! What are you doing here?" she demanded, "and how did you get past security? This is a restricted area."

"I'm sorry; I don't mean to intrude. I snuck past the guardians because I have come to apologize."

"Apologize?" Haley asked, doubtfully.

"Yes. I realize I must have seemed totally insensitive when you came to the infirmary the other day."

"Now that you mention it . . . " Haley retorted. "I was this close to knocking you into next week," she said, holding up her thumb and index finger, forming an inch.

"I'm sorry?" Violet asked, not understanding.

"I mean, I felt like punching you right in the face," Haley said, loudly.

"Punching?"

"Oh, never mind."

"Honest Haley, I am so sorry. I didn't realize that you and Valian were close."

Before Haley could interrupt, she continued.

"Really, I take my work very seriously and thought I was acting in Sir Valian's best interest."

She sounded sincere, but Haley's intuition told her Violet was a fake. *"Two can play this game,"* she thought to herself. *I can be just as devious, even more so because I'm human."* She smiled at Violet.

"I'm sorry too," she said. "Sorry, we got off on the wrong foot."

Violet seemed to relax and looked a little more confident with herself as she gave Haley another fake smile.

"So, we're okay then?" Violet asked, with a sweet, innocent look.

"Of course we are," Haley replied, putting a friendly arm around Violet's shoulders.

Violet flinched, just slightly. Haley felt it but didn't let on.

"Come on," Haley continued, "let's start over. So . . . how long have you been with the infirmary?"

"Sometimes it seems like forever," Violet answered with a sigh.

She talked to Haley as if they had been friends for years, chattering, making small talk.

Haley saw right through it. She had major suspicions and remembered Valian's words about trusting and not trusting.

Violet went on and on about nothing in particular when she suddenly saw the ruby chain on Haley's wrist.

"Oh my, that is gorgeous!" She exclaimed. "It looks . . . well, it looks like a betrothal bracelet," she laughed nervously.

Haley looked down at the bracelet with a triumphant smile. "Valian gave it to me just this morning."

She enjoyed the defeat displayed on Violet's face as she continued.

"Yes, we went for a sail, and you know, one thing led to another, and he asked me to marry him."

She looked at Violet with an innocent smile of her own.

"Well . . . congratulations," Violet muttered, at a loss for words.

"Thank you," Haley replied nonchalantly. "So . . . I really must be going. Valian is announcing our engagement at dinner, and I really shouldn't be late."

"Oh, of course . . . I . . . I'll just be off now. I am so glad we got the chance to talk," she continued.

She was talking so fast, babbling nervously as Haley ushered her into the corridor.

"Thank you for stopping by. We'll have to do this again real soon," she said, shutting the door.

Haley let out a huge sigh as the latch clicked.

"For goodness sakes," she said aloud. "She's not very bright."

She took Sarah's necklace from her peach gown and placed it in her pocket. She knew Valian would have already invited the Bonners to their special dinner and she couldn't wait to give it back to Sarah.

She looked in the mirror one more time and went toward the door just as she heard another knock.

She rolled her eyes.

"Who is it?"

"Your escort, milady."

With a sigh of relief, she opened the door.

A tall, rather skinny steward stood at attention.

She flashed him a smile. "I'm ready."

Chapter Five

CREATURE MADNESS

Haley followed her escort down the hall. Her heart was so light; she felt she was almost floating.

He led her to a small dining room. It was lavishly decorated with all things white. Pure white draperies tied back with red silk; braided ropes adorned the large arched windows.

"The white shag carpet was enhanced with smaller red rugs strategically placed. Pedestal tables were arranged around two large white sofas that faced each other, loaded down with red pillows.

In front of a huge bay window was a table laden with a crisp, white linen tablecloth, set for seven.

Beautiful white china dishes edged in gold and gold goblets sparkled in the sunshine pouring into the room. Everything gleamed.

The fireplace stood empty and clean. Silk curtains separated the dining area from the rest of the room, and the candelabras flickering on the pedestal tables and the light scent of lilac brought a serene atmosphere.

In the far corner of the room were four high-backed, red velvet chairs where Zeb and Sarah sat talking quietly. They were all smiles as Haley entered the room.

"Zeb, Sarah," she greeted them, giving Sarah a hug. "I am so glad to see you."

"Prince Valian came to see us and invited us to what he called a special dinner," said Zeb, helping Haley to a chair.

"Before I forget," said Haley, reaching into her pocket. "I have something that belongs to you."

She pulled out the ruby necklace and passed it to Sarah.

"Oh, my goodness!" Sarah exclaimed with excitement. "I never thought to see this again!"

Zeb looked at Haley with amazement and apprehension.

She looked back at him with a look that said, "Don't worry."

Haley found the necklace and a wedding dress in the coffin Zeb built for Sarah when he was sure she had drowned in the Kootenai River, along with their two little daughters, Susan and Rosie. Haley was sure he didn't want the fact mentioned that he buried three empty coffins on the grounds of the estate.

Sarah held it up to the light, admiring it. "Darling . . . could you?" she asked, handing the necklace to her husband.

Zeb fastened the clasp around her neck.

"Wherever did you find . . . " Sarah began, as the door opened and Valian and Henry came in, much to Haley and Zeb's relief.

"Zeb, Sarah," said Henry, walking over to shake Zeb's hand.

Queen Lilia came in just behind them with Sersha.

Everyone gathered in the corner greeting each other, commenting on the great weather and how the children were doing.

Reed appeared out of nowhere and announced that dinner was served.

The group gathered at the table as several brownies dressed in fine attire like little black and white tuxedos brought out large steaming platters of food. Bowing to each of the party as they made their way around the table, they served up fine steaks smothered in sautéed onions and mushrooms.

A sparkling concoction fizzed in the golden goblets as Valian stood to propose a toast.

"Welcome. Thank you for coming."

He looked at Haley glowing beside him and took her hand. "Haley, please rise."

As she stood, Sersha let out a small gasp as she spotted Haley's bracelet.

The queen followed her gaze, and a smile came over her face. "It's about time!" she exclaimed, rising from her chair, raising her goblet.

The others stood up, looking from the queen to Valian, confused.

"Yes," said Valian, with the biggest smile. "I have asked Haley to marry me. We are betrothed!"

Everyone clapped and laughed with joy while Henry stood there silent with his mouth hanging open.

"Married?" he asked, in shock.

"Well, not right away," said Valian, as Zeb shook his hand. "We must be betrothed for three years before we can wed."

Henry looked from Valian to Haley.

"It's alright, Henry, we're only engaged," she said, smiling.

Henry had a peculiar look on his face, almost like he'd lost his best friend.

She knew at once what he was thinking. They had been together all their lives, sharing everything. Now there was someone else in her life. She would marry and move away, leaving him alone. The special connection that twins have would be broken.

Henry's mood was somber.

The queen, Valian, and Sersha didn't see what had just happened between the twins and went on celebrating.

"We must make an announcement and plan the engagement gala at once," said Lilia, excitedly.

The rest of the meal was filled with excited chatter except for Henry. Haley participated in the conversation with nervous laughter as she stole glances at him. He hadn't even touched his food. She decided she was going to have a long talk with him, and soon.

Reed suddenly appeared out of nowhere as usual and began clearing the table as the group stood.

"Let's go out onto the terrace and enjoy some cocktails and continue our discussion for the betrothal gala," said the queen, opening the door.

As she finished her suggestion, Reed froze in his tracks, just for a moment. Long enough for Haley to catch it, then he continued to clear the dishes. It gave her a very uncomfortable feeling.

As they entered the hall, Henry apologized, saying he was tired and was going back to his room, taking Haley by surprise.

"Are you sure?" she asked him.

"Yeah, I'm beat," he said, heading in the opposite direction.

They gathered on the terrace, and Haley listened as Sersha and the queen made plans; all the while, her mind was back to Henry.

They retired an hour later.

Haley went to bed and fell into a troubled sleep.

Violet paced the floor back and forth, mumbling to herself. She was furious.

"What am I going to do now?" she said aloud. "How could he be betrothed to that . . . that human?"

If her anger had been visible, it would have filled her entire cottage. She was seething.

Violet stopped suddenly, whacking her forehead with the heel of her hand. She was so overcome with hatred for Haley and the announcement of the betrothal, she had completely forgotten about the love potion.

Quickly she retrieved the little box Maximillion had given her and the Peruvian toadstools and sat down at her small table.

With a wave of her hand, a small lantern appeared, lighting the area in a dull glow.

Opening the box, she poured the black glittering powder into the small wooden bowl. As she picked up one of the toadstools, she noticed it had shriveled up and was now a grayish color.

Shrugging her shoulders, she added the toadstools and began mashing them with a fork. Almost immediately the concoction liquefied into a thick, black, tar like substance. She grimaced at the sight.

"How am I supposed to drink that?" she said to herself.

The mixture smelled horrible. She plugged her nose and raised the bowl to her lips. She took a deep breath and swallowed the entire thing in one gulp.

The effects were instantly apparent. Her face grew hot, and it felt like her ears were on fire. The heat radiated down her neck and across her chest. She began to feel a prickly sensation all over her body, and she began to itch.

Fear swept over her, and she ran to the mirror. She showed no signs of any physical change, but she continued to itch terribly.

As she began to scratch, small welts appeared. Horrified, she ran into her bathroom and stood under a cold shower, which gave her some relief.

After about twenty minutes, the itching stopped. She climbed out of the shower and checked the mirror again. The welts were gone, and so was the heat. Relieved, she giggled.

"What a weird reaction," she said aloud, shrugging her shoulders. "Now, I must sneak into the castle and let the prince see me. He'll fall madly in love with me and tell that little twit human to go home!" she laughed.

She didn't realize how much time had passed, and by the time she got to the castle everyone had already gone to bed.

The guardians were on duty at all the entrances, and she knew there was no use in sticking around. She would just have to wait until morning.

With an angry snap of her wings, she took off into the starry night.

Haley woke, dressed, and headed toward the courtyard without waiting for her steward.

It was a sunny, crisp morning. The dew sparkled like little diamonds on the wet leaves. She wanted to get there early so she could talk with Henry in private.

The courtyard was deserted. 'It must be really early,' she thought to herself.

She sat at one of the tables and thought about what she would say to her brother, how she might put him at ease with the idea of the engagement.

She heard a shuffling behind her and turned to see several brownies bringing out dishes to set the tables.

She got up and went to the balcony. Looking out over the city in the treetops, she marveled at how beautiful this place was. Plumes of smoke began to rise all over the forest as fairy families began their day.

Looking down to the forest floor far below, the lanterns that fed the flowers with light began to flicker as bright sunbeams streamed through the canopy.

She turned toward her left to view the grounds and was startled to see Sersha standing beside her.

She gasped and clutched her chest. "Oh, my gosh! You scared me!"

"Sorry," said Sersha with a gentle smile. "I noticed you as I passed the first arch. Are you okay?"

"I'm okay. It's just that . . . well, Henry didn't take the announcement of the betrothal very well."

"Really? He looked alright to me. How could you tell?"

"I could see it in his eyes and his demeanor."

"I don't understand, Sersha replied. His eyes looked normal to me. What do you mean?"

"I guess you have to be a human to see it."

"Good morning, ladies," Valian called as he approached.

They turned and Haley beamed at him.

"My sweet," he said, kissing her hand. "So . . . what was up with Henry yesterday? He was acting strangely and didn't even eat."

Haley looked at Valian in surprise, as did Sersha.

"How could you tell?" Sersha asked.

"I don't know. It was his eyes, and he seemed distant."

Haley's mouth dropped open.

"How could you tell? How could you see that?" Sersha asked, astounded.

"Yeah?" Haley agreed.

"Well, it was obvious to me. Couldn't you two see it?"

"Haley could but I couldn't," Sersha answered, worry in her voice. "Maybe you should get a check-up at the infirmary."

"I feel fine," he said, with enthusiasm, "and I'm starved. Let's get some breakfast. Are you ready?"

As they sat down, the brownies emerged with trays filled with all sorts of delights. There were fruit trays, pastries, and a variety of cereals, plus the usual eggs, bacon and ham.

Haley helped herself to some fruit and toast and ate quietly, waiting for Henry.

Valian and Sersha chatted about the upcoming betrothal gala while she kept watching the arched doors, but Henry was nowhere in sight.

A soft gong sounded, and Queen Lilia hurried toward them. Haley knew at once something was wrong.

"What's wrong, Mother?" Valian asked, rising from the table.

Again, Haley and Sersha exchanged puzzled looks.

"Come with me," the queen urged.

They retreated to the living room and sat down on the blue sofas, waiting for the queen to explain.

"Something is happening to the bulwarks. They seem to have gone somewhat berserk."

The group exchanged looks as Lilia continued.

"They have gone crazy or something!"

"How do you mean?" Valian asked.

"They've deserted their posts and are running amuck. I have had reports that the gloaming varieties are stalking all manner of creatures just this morning. Gloaming varieties are the kind that wanders in the night," she explained, seeing Haley's confusion. "They never come out during the day!"

"Have they hurt anyone?" Sersha asked.

"Not that I am aware of, not yet, but they were spotted stabbing their stalks into the water and scattering the Bocan fish, scaring them to death. And the mermaids are afraid to come out to sun themselves. I don't know what's happened to them. Oh, and to top it all off, a batch of dwindle drops has been reported missing."

"Oh my!" Sersha whispered.

"I don't know what's going on, but we must investigate this at once!" exclaimed the queen. "We'll send out every available guardian."

"This worries me," said Valian, "and really makes me mad that someone would steal dwindle drops. You know how dangerous they could be in someone else's hands?"

Lilia gave him an odd look.

Haley couldn't hold back the question any longer. "What has happened to you?" she asked.

"What do you mean?"

"Well, these emotions you're feeling, I've never noticed them so pronounced."

"Now that you mention it," said the queen, "you displayed some unusual emotion at the witches' council meeting too."

Everyone looked at him as if his ears had suddenly quadrupled in size.

"I don't know," he answered with a puzzled look. "I've been feeling a bit different since I woke up in the infirmary."

Haley thought for a moment. "How did you feel before the attack?" she asked.

"Like my normal self."

"Then something must have happened during the attack to give you this ability. Is there anything physically different that you can tell?"

"Only my appetite."

"That's odd. Your eating habits are just like Henry's. Hmm," said Haley, drumming her fingers on the coffee table. "Was there anything unusual with the clothes you had on?"

"No," he answered, scratching his head.

"Well, I can't think of anything else . . . except your injury. Let me see where you were stabbed."

Valian pulled open his tunic to show a zipper shaped scar on his chest.

"Where is your given gem?" Sersha inquired.

Valian felt over his neck and chest.

"I . . . I don't know. I didn't realize it was gone."

"That may be it," Haley exclaimed excitedly. "What was your given gem?"

"It is a diamond."

She sat quietly deep in thought. Finally, she broke the silence.

"It almost seems that the qualities granted from a given gem diminish when absent. You are exhibiting more and more human qualities without it. It's like . . . your gem has protected you somehow. Maybe that is why you needed human help to rescue Zeb because you were unable to experience full-blown emotions and put them to use fully."

Haley looked at the queen.

"Have the fairies always worn given gems?"

"As far as I know," Lilia answered with a strange look.

"That's got to be it!" Haley responded. "Your given gems have protected you from the beginning. That's why Roan seems so peaceful and serene to you."

"Yeah!" said Sersha. "Remember at the witches' council meeting, you were angry?"

"And jealous," added the queen.

"Jealous?" Haley asked, looking at Valian.

Valian's face turned a light shade of red.

"Look! He's blushing!" she insisted with excitement.

The queen and Sersha didn't understand.

"He's embarrassed!" Haley giggled.

Sersha and Lilia shook their heads.

Valian turned away with a grin.

"We experience emotion," stated the queen, "just not as much as you. We laugh, we are saddened when bad things happen, and we get frustrated when we don't understand. So you're saying, given gems suppress our emotion, that we could experience the same level of emotions as humans?"

"Yes . . . yes you can!" Haley answered. She was thrilled with this discovery. "Take off your gems," she commanded, looking at Sersha and Lilia.

They looked at her apprehensively.

"We've never taken them off before. What's going to happen?" Lilia asked. "Are we going to act weird?"

Haley laughed. "No. You'll just be the same two people you already are."

Sersha and the queen removed their gems. They looked at each other, making sure nothing had changed. After they were certain they were still normal they were all smiles.

Valian gave them a reassuring nod.

"You know this may really help to cope with what's happening lately. If we put our heads together, we can solve the mysteries," said Haley. "I'm sure of it."

"Well, I hope so," said the queen. "Now, let's assemble the guardians and try to figure out what's going on."

"Have them all remove their given gems," said Haley.

"Yes," Valian agreed.

The queen sent out messengers to call the guardians to assemble at once in the great dining room. Thirty minutes later, she called the meeting to order.

The guardians were told to remove their gems and put them away for safekeeping and then were instructed to go out and observe the bulwarks.

One guardian was asked to go to Bella's Blossom Shop to speak to the owner and find out everything there was to know about the plant.

Valian, Sersha, and Haley were going to walk the forest floor to make sure there weren't any bulwarks wreaking havoc.

As they finished the meeting, Haley was really starting to worry about Henry. When they passed by the great archways, she spotted him on the terrace having a late breakfast. She excused herself, telling the others she wanted to speak to Henry alone.

Henry looked up as she approached and gave her a half-hearted smile.

"Congratulations," he said. "I'm sorry about yesterday. I think I was just in shock."

"That's alright," she said, giving him a hug.

"I think it's cool you're going to be a princess; I just feel worried."

"About what?"

"About the future, you not being around anymore."

"Gee Henry, I'm not leaving you. You're still my brother and I want you to be in my life, always."

Henry grinned.

"I know; it's just that things will be different."

"Yes, I guess they will be, but that's three years from now, and who knows what can happen in three years? Maybe you'll find yourself a sweetheart."

Henry grinned again and turned red in the face.

"Speaking of blushing," she said, "we think we've figured out what has been happening to Valian." She related the conversation they had with the queen at the guardian meeting.

"Wow, do you really think that's it?" Henry asked.

"Absolutely. Are you going to come with us?"

"Yes, I'm ready," he answered, finishing the last of his breakfast.

Valian and Sersha came out onto the terrace wearing their swords.

Valian handed Henry his bow and a quiver of arrows.

"You'll have to be a good shot," said Valian. "Bulwarks are big in size, but they are extremely agile."

"We're not going to kill them?" Henry asked, alarmed.

"Not if we can help it," Valian answered. "Bulwarks have been known to be vicious at times. It's just a precaution."

Haley remembered Hilda telling her about being attacked by a bulwark.

"Do you have a weapon for me?" she asked.

Sersha handed her a slender silver sword. It was sharp and gleaming with a pearl white handle.

"Have you ever used one of these before?" Sersha asked.

"No, but I've seen it done."

"It takes many years of practice to become skilled," said Sersha. "Perhaps Valian can teach you the basics before we go."

Valian smiled at Haley.

"It will be my pleasure, milady," he bowed.

So right then and there, Valian gave Haley instructions on how to block a strike. She caught on quickly, and he commented on her quick reflexes.

"Excellent! You're a natural! With more practice I think you'll be a fine swordsman . . . woman," he grinned.

Henry was impressed, marveling at her ability.

"I think your being human has given you an edge," said Valian. "You'll be an outstanding guardian someday."

Haley smiled and was amazed at how she was able to anticipate Valian's moves. She thought the classes in martial arts she took in school probably had something to do with it.

An hour later they were flying toward the forest floor where they paired up.

They were silent as they traveled down the well worn paths. Haley was again delighted at the abundance of flowers and was so taken by the sweet fragrance that she had to remind herself why they were there.

They peeked around the giant tree trunks, checking around corners of the many gardening sheds, but didn't see a thing. As they approached the edge of the forest they looked out over an open meadow.

The morning sun lit up the meadow in vivid colors. Emerald green grasses swayed in the breeze, and the flowers that grew there took Haley's breath away.

Groups of giant sunflowers with bright yellow heads stood tall and proud as bees buzzed around them in such frenzy as they fought each other for the nectar. Huge butterflies flit into view, flying with no specific destination.

Haley drew in a deep breath and sighed.

"Your world is just incredible."

"Well, there's nothing going on here," said Valian. "Shall we continue on? We should really check the mermaid pools."

Everyone nodded in agreement.

As they made their way across the meadow, Haley looked down at the patch of brilliant purple flowers they were walking through. They were very small and delicate and smelled wonderful.

She heard very faint sounds coming from them and stopped to bend down to get a closer look.

"Ouch!" she yelled in surprise.

The others stopped and turned around.

"It stung me!" she said, reaching down to scratch her ankle.

At that moment, all the other flowers in the patch began talking quietly at first, then louder and louder until the others could hear them.

"Get out of our patch! You don't belong here! Get out!" They were all yelling and reaching out their thorn-covered stems, trying to stab at their ankles.

Valian and Henry began jumping up and down from one foot to the other, yelling.

"Ouch! Ow!"

Haley began to laugh at the comical scene before her.

Sersha was suddenly jabbed in the exposed area of her sandaled foot.

"Ow!" she yelled.

They began to run, tripping over the stems as they stretched out, trying to exert as many pokes as they could.

The foursome took flight.

Henry let out a yelp. One of the flowers had him by the foot. Its stems were wrapped around it, stabbing his ankle and yelling at him as the rest of the flowers joined in with continuous cussing and yelling.

Valian pulled his sword and cut the stem. It let out a scream of anger and shrank back to the ground, swearing up a storm.

The sound of cursing flowers faded as they flew toward the mermaid pools.

Haley was still laughing as they landed on the bank.

Henry was chuckling, while Valian and Sersha grinned, rubbing their ankles.

"What in the world was that all about?" Haley asked. "Are they always that way?"

"No," Sersha answered. "I've never seen them act like that before. And why were they so small? Do you suppose the same thing that happened to the bulwarks is happening to them?"

"I don't know, maybe," Valian answered.

They gazed out over the mermaid pool, and all was silent. Not a mermaid in sight, not a glint of silver fish scales or the slap of a tail.

"This is peculiar," said Valian. "I wonder where they've gone."

They watched the pool for twenty minutes but saw nothing except an occasional minnow swimming by and dragonflies skimming the surface.

"Not much going on here either," said Sersha, turning to go.

"Prince Valian! Prince Valian!"

They looked up as one of the guardians flew toward them.

"Prince Valian, look!"

He opened his hand as he landed, and squirming in his palm was the tiniest bulwark Valian had ever seen.

"What?" Valian exclaimed, "What is this?"

"It's a bulwark," the guardian answered.

"I know it's a bulwark!"

Haley giggled.

"But what's happened to it?"

"We don't know. We were hiking just past the outskirts when we ran into a whole pack of them."

The bulwark was slashing its tiny branches into the palm of the guardian's hand and trying to sink its little claws and teeth into him.

"Oh, he's so cute," laughed Haley, reaching down to pet it.

It latched onto her finger and proceeded to bite her.

She jerked her hand and the bulwark flew through the air, landing a few feet away and promptly scurried into the bushes.

Valian gave her an amused look and turned toward the guardian.

"We must report this at once and check with the guardian that went to Bella's."

They arrived a short time later at the palace.

Upon hearing the news about the flowers and the tiny bulwarks, a look of understanding came over the queen's face.

"It's the dwindle drops," she said. "The missing dwindle drops. Somehow the bulwarks must have gotten hold of them."

The group was puzzled about this.

"You know they'll eat just about anything," she continued. "Dwindle drops are not meant to be consumed by plant life. Now we know how they are affected. They can shrink in size, and it makes them crazy. Thankfully the affects are not permanent."

"Valian, you told us that once you eat one dwindle drop, you never have to eat another. I thought they were permanent."

"Your drops were charmed, so you would never have to eat another," Valian replied.

"So, the condition won't last for the plants?" Haley asked, looking at the queen.

"Who can tell? This has never happened before," Lilia answered. "And somehow, the flowers were exposed as well. This is not good. Who knows who or what else has had access to the dwindle drops."

"Well, it doesn't seem to have harmed them," said Haley, "just made them a little nuts. It'll probably just wear off."

"We'll have to keep an eye on them and hope for the best," said the queen.

Sersha suggested they go out to the terrace for some lunch.

Just as they arrived, a cloud covered the sun, and the wind began to pick up. A storm was fast approaching. Soon, the sky was filled with clouds.

As the minutes passed, the sky turned a dark blue-gray color. Gusts of wind began to blow debris around and flocks of birds were scattered in mid flight. The sound of thunder rumbled in the distance as the storm grew closer.

They stood in the arched doorway looking up at the sky. Leaves flew past as the wind grew stronger, and the first strike of lightning flashed across the sky.

Haley looked up at the dark clouds, watching as they churned in all different directions. She had seen clouds like this before, and she urged the others to come inside, but they just stood there, transfixed.

They could see sheets of rain in the distance, blurring out everything as it got darker. Lightning lit up the sky, striking the ground, and the crack of rolling thunder followed.

Haley was becoming extremely anxious. She'd always enjoyed a good thunderstorm, but this was becoming dangerous. She was fearful. She had seen tornadoes develop from storms like these on TV.

The wind began to blow so hard that their hair was standing almost straight out from their heads.

Haley was just about to call out to them again when a large tree branch crashed onto the terrace. That got everybody moving.

They retreated into the great dining hall as the first large drops of rain began to hit the windows. Small hail balls bounced on the terrace in every direction. Debris began to hit the castle. They could hear the thumping and crashing of unknown objects as they landed.

Suddenly, Hilda blew through the great arch. Her hair, cloak, and broomstick were all askew.

"Good heavens!" she exclaimed, brushing her wet hair off her face.

Everyone stood silent, startled by her sudden appearance.

"Sorry," she apologized. "I was on the way back from visiting Norman and Mable when this horrible wind came up and blew me clean out of the outskirts," she said, brushing the leaves and twigs off her clothes. "What is up with these storms lately? I've never seen storms like these before. What do you think, your majesty?"

Lilia shook her head. "I don't know. I think it's Molock. These storms are moving in from his direction. And it is possible he may have something to do with the dwindle drops as well. Unlikely, but possible."

There was almost a hint of panic in Lilia's voice, and though these were scary events, Haley smiled to herself. The removal of the given gems seemed to be working. The queen was showing fear, which she was incapable of feeling a couple of hours ago.

They followed her to the blue sofa room.

"I don't like this feeling," said Lilia, sinking into a chair.

"It's alright," said Haley, going to her. "Fear is a natural emotion when one is uncertain about things," she said in a comforting voice. "You have to look beyond that fear and concentrate on the task at hand. Overlook it. Ignore it. Fear can also sharpen your senses and reactions if you can learn to control it."

Lilia looked at her. "So, this is a good thing?"

"It can be. I will teach you. I'll teach you to understand these emotions, how to cope with them, embrace them, and use them to your advantage."

Lilia looked a bit relieved.

Sersha and Valian just sat and listened to Haley's logic. They didn't get it yet but were eager to learn.

Thunder cracked loudly, echoing across the land as it raced toward an unknown destination, making everyone jump, even the twins.

"You see!" said Haley. "It startled me as much as it did you. It's just a reaction. It can't hurt you."

Lilia let out a half giggle, half sigh.

"It is a bit exhilarating, isn't it?"

Haley smiled and nodded, patting her on the shoulder.

"It is indeed," she agreed.

The winds continued to blow, and the thunder and lightning played tag long into the night. The rain cooled things off in a hurry, and soon, fires were crackling in hearths across the land.

Fairies were gathered in small groups, in pubs and living rooms, discussing the unusual weather.

Queen Lilia and the rest of the group sat beside the fireplace in the beautiful room with the blue sofas and chatted about the day's strange events; experiencing new emotions, the dwindle drop mystery, and the phantom apprentice.

"How are we going to discover the identity of the apprentice and his purpose?" Lilia was saying as Reed entered the room.

"Yes Reed?" she acknowledged.

"Would Your Highness care to dine in here this evening?" he asked.

He was speaking to the queen, but his eyes darted to Haley for a moment, then back to the queen.

Haley had had it with this brownie and his odd behavior. She stood and walked toward him.

Reed bowed slightly and took a step backward.

"What is it with you?" she demanded.

Everyone stopped talking and turned to watch.

"I beg your pardon, milady?" he asked in a calm, cool tone.

Queen Lilia looked at Haley and turned to Reed.

"Well?" she said, not really knowing why she said it.

"Ever since I arrived here, you have been giving me strange looks every time you come in, and I don't like it. So, what gives?" Haley demanded.

"I know not what you mean, milady."

Haley sighed deeply. This wasn't going to be easy. Trying to get something out of a brownie was proving to be difficult.

"You make me uncomfortable when you come in here staring at me all the time."

"Please forgive milady," he replied, bowing. "I am smitten by your beauty and humanness."

Haley was taken by surprise at his words.

"I . . . I'm sorry, I misunderstood," she apologized. She was, however, not quite convinced but decided to drop it for now and went back to the fire and sat down on one of the cushy chaise lounge chairs.

Haley sat quietly, watching as Reed began to set the table.

Moments later, several brownies came in loaded down with food. The fried chicken was on the evening menu, along with a variety of vegetables, including Haley's favorite, corn on the cob.

The smell of freshly baked bread made her mouth water. She hadn't realized how hungry she was. Her breakfast had been interrupted by the queen that morning, and now she felt famished.

The table was quiet as everyone dished up their plates and began eating.

"We'll announce the betrothal tomorrow morning at breakfast," said Lilia, between mouthfuls. "I'll send out the messengers to invite the entire kingdom."

Haley paused, watching everyone eat. She had never seen the queen or Valian, and Sersha shoveled it in so fast. She smiled again to herself as the evidence of emotion was as plain as the nose on her face.

Their appetites were changing. She looked over at Henry. He had paused also to watch the others and grinned at her.

They finished dinner, and everyone stretched out on the chaise lounge chairs and pillows on the floor by the fire.

Reed cleared the table and came back with after-dinner drinks.

"Umm," Haley sighed, "ember potion."

The wind died down somewhat, but thunder and lightning continued as they sipped their drinks.

Valian pulled up a lounge chair next to Haley, and they held hands as Lilia and Sersha continued discussing the upcoming gala. The couple sat quietly listening, enjoying the comfortable silence and the crackle of the fire.

Hilda stood and stretched. "Well, I thank you for your hospitality and sanctuary and the delicious meal, but I must fly. At least the wind has subsided a bit," she added.

Valian got up. "I'll escort you out," he said, politely.

"Thank you, Sir Valian."

Haley watched them go and thought to herself how respectful and kind Valian was.

"I am going to weave a special gown for you," said Sersha. "It's going to be fabulous. I'll also make a tunic for Valian."

Lilia nodded her approval.

One by one, they began to nod off.

The stewards had been patiently waiting for their charges to call it a night and took it upon themselves to suggest everyone go to bed.

Chapter Six

THE BETRAYAL OF ROAN

The storm hadn't let up the next morning. It was still lightning and thundering but not as fierce. The sky was a dark gray, and the steady drizzle made everything cool and damp. The terrace was empty as Haley was escorted past the great arches.

The great dining hall was totally packed with fairies standing in groups, and the tables were filling up quickly.

Haley spotted Henry and Valian seated at the head of the queen's table, laughing up a storm.

"What's so funny?" she asked, approaching the chair next to Valian.

He rose and kissed her hand. "We were just talking about the flower bed from yesterday."

"Now that was funny," she smiled, looking around. "Man, it's crowded in here. Who are all these fairies?"

"Mother invited them for the announcement. Twenty percent are with the royal court, the rest are citizens."

Haley spotted Violet at the far end of the room, surrounded by several burly males. She laughed sweetly at whatever they were saying as she watched Haley and Valian out of the corner of her eye. She was being just a little louder than necessary, as if trying to get Valian's attention.

Haley took Valian's hand in hers, making sure her betrothal bracelet was clearly visible.

Violet's face grew red, and her gracious movements became stiff and jerky.

Haley could see the twisted rage on her face. She flashed Violet a triumphant smile

Violet's wings began to twitch, like a nervous tick.

Haley giggled and turned to Valian, giving him her complete attention, although she couldn't resist the temptation to steal glances at her rival.

Sersha joined them a short time later. "I'm starving," she said. "Where is Mother?"

The crowd began to grow restless. Fairies began taking their seats, watching the doorway expectantly. After another twenty minutes passed without a sign of the queen, Valian suggested they get started.

"She must be tied up with something. Shall we go ahead?" he asked, looking at Sersha.

Sersha nodded, and he stood.

"Sorry for the delay; everyone, obviously, the queen is held up. Let's begin."

The brownies entered, and breakfast began. As those in attendance finished eating, Valian stood again.

"Does anyone have anything that needs to be addressed?"

A large red-headed fairy wearing a bronze breastplate and a dark blue tunic rose into the air about two feet.

"Yes, I would like to know what is to be done about the bulwarks. They have torn up my brother's crop of beans, chewing holes in every one. The crop is ruined."

Another fairy hovered next to him.

"Not only that, but my bee hives are in trouble. The bees have shrunk in size and aren't putting out the usual amount of honey. What has happened to them?"

Two more fairies rose at the same time and began asking questions, then two more and two more. Soon, dozens were in the air, asking questions and demanding answers.

"We have a riot on our hands," Haley thought to herself.

As Valian raised his hand to try and quiet them down, the gong sounded, and everyone sank back to their seats. Silence swept across the room as if someone had flicked a switch.

Queen Lilia entered the room with a very serious look. "Everyone, we have a crisis. The sacred sphere has been stolen!"

The room erupted with gasps. Fairies covered their mouths in shock. Many rose out of their seats in disbelief.

"How can this be? I thought the sphere was protected," said a fairy sitting next to Valian.

"It was," the queen replied. "The guardians in charge of its protection are missing."

Again, the room grew loud with questions. A female fairy with long dark hair began to tremble and cry.

Haley looked at the queen, concerned.

"Alright everyone, please calm down! Quiet please," said the queen loudly. "It's alright. We will deal with this situation. This is obviously most serious, but do not worry. We will catch the culprits. We have the best minds to assist us," she said, motioning to the twins. "Haley, do you wish to address the group?"

Haley was taken aback for a moment. She hadn't expected to have to teach everyone, at least not all at once. She rose into the air so she could be seen and heard by all.

Valian beamed up at her in anticipation.

"Ah hem," she cleared her throat. "Can everyone hear me okay?"

There were nods the room.

"Queen Lilia is quite right when she asked you all to be calm. I know this latest incident is critical. Any fear you may be experiencing is a natural reaction, but you must rise above it and keep a clear head."

She looked around the room at all the anxious faces staring up at her, and her heart felt for them.

"Fear has its place," she continued. "It helps you become a bit wary of some things, which is good. It can also help keep you on your toes and alert, but don't waste time agonizing over this situation. It will not help in finding the sphere, and rest assured we will find it. It didn't disappear into thin air."

Looking over the crowd, she saw them beginning to relax a bit, and she smiled at them all.

"Don't worry; things have a way of working themselves out. Now I want everyone to take a deep breath and let it out slowly, then turn to the one beside you and give them a hug."

Everyone followed her instruction, and soon, fairies were breaking out in smiles and soft laughter.

Queen Lilia rose from her seat.

"Thank you, Haley. Your instruction is sound and wise. You are a kindred spirit. Alright, everyone, you will do well to heed Haley's advice; also, quickly, I called you all here for an announcement, Valian . . ."

Valian's face grew red as he rose. He made it short and sweet.

"Haley and I are betrothed!"

Cheers broke out all over the room.

"In light of recent events, the betrothal gala will have to be postponed until we have solved this mystery!" he yelled over the crowd.

His yelling made no difference. The cheers continued.

Fairies swarmed the couple with congratulations and claps on the back.

As the excitement began to die down, some fairies sat back down and others left the dining hall.

The group went to the living room, which Haley decided to name, the blue room, with Valian's approval. After taking their seats, they began to brainstorm.

"Tell me about these two guardians," said Haley.

"Well," Valian began. "They're cousins. I recruited them myself about a century ago. They were in the guardian academy together and were extremely fit. Their performance was exemplary."

"Where did they come from?" Haley asked. "Do you know?"

"I'm not sure exactly, somewhere down south, I believe. The land is vast but I think they may have come from one of the islands."

"We should probably take a look at the scene of the crime."

"I agree," said Lilia, "but first I need to eat. I'm famished. Where is Reed?" she asked.

"I don't know," Valian replied. "I didn't see him at breakfast."

Haley raised an eyebrow. "Really," she stated. "Now, why doesn't that surprise me?"

The others looked at her and understood at once.

"Maybe your suspicions were correct," said Valian. "Reed has never been absent at any meal. He has always been punctual."

"Maybe he is sick," Henry suggested. "We should check his quarters."

"You check his quarters while I go to the kitchen for a bite," said Lilia.

Valian led the way to Reed's quarters located directly behind the queen's bedroom. He knocked. There was no answer. He knocked again, louder this time. Nothing but silence answered. He tried the door, and it was unlocked.

He entered. The room was dark, and he waved his hand. Half a dozen lanterns lit the room. The place was in shambles. Dresser drawers were left open with their contents gone. Papers and all manner of trash were strewn all over. The closet door stood ajar, and the closet was empty.

"What a slob!" Sersha said in disgust as she walked in.

"It looks like he left in a hurry," said Haley, picking up a pile of papers from the bed. "What's this?" she exclaimed.

"What?" Valian asked, walking over to her.

"It's a newspaper from Spokane. How did Reed get his hands on this?"

"He doesn't have authority to use the portals," said Valian.

"Then how did he get it?" Henry asked.

"Either someone gave it to him, or he has found a way to the other side," Haley answered.

"Oh dear," Sersha said, quietly.

The others looked at her.

"You don't suppose he aided in the theft of the sphere and has taken it there?"

Valian gave her a look of alarm.

"If he did, wouldn't the trip through a portal damage or destroy the sphere? It's so fragile," Haley said.

"Oh, my gosh!" Sersha whispered. "That would be dreadful. Roan needs the sphere. It is sacred. It holds the mysteries of our land. It can be a dangerous tool. I don't know how long we can endure without it," she shuddered.

"I think it unlikely the sphere is on the other side," said Haley, looking down at the newspaper. "I am wondering if they have used the sphere for time travel! Look at this paper. It has tomorrow's date. They must have stolen the sphere last night after we went to bed, then went to the other side and came back again. That doesn't make sense. Why come back at all?"

"I know," Henry answered.

Everyone looked at him.

"It's a plant. They're trying to trick us into thinking they are on the other side, but they are not very bright, are they."

Haley smiled at him.

"I'll bet you're right, brother dear. Maybe they have been sneaking to the other side all along when no one is around, like during meetings and meal times. Or maybe the sphere wasn't stolen last night. When was the last time you saw it?" she asked Valian.

"Weeks," he answered. "We'll check with Mother and find out when she saw it last."

Henry was busy looking around the room when he spotted a piece of paper poking out from under the mattress. He pulled it out.

"Well, looky here," he said as he unfolded it.

It was an elaborate drawing of a map, very detailed.

Everyone gathered around him to have a look.

"I don't recognize any of this, but look," said Valian, growing excited, "islands! See, I knew it!"

"We'll have to take a trip," said Haley. "It's obvious that's where they've taken the sphere. Henry's right. This was just a ploy to throw us off track and going in the wrong direction," she said, throwing the newspaper down on the bed.

Henry pocketed the map.

"Let's go have a look in the sacred chamber," he said.

Valian led the way through the halls, down the long corridors to the hallway full of doors. With a wave of his hand, one of the tall, skinny doors opened, and they entered. He shook his head at the sight.

The room was just as Haley remembered. Dimly lit, heavily draped, with high back chairs all facing the north wall. There before them was the empty space where the sacred sphere used to sit, supported by a round wooden brace.

"How could they have possibly gotten it out of here?" Haley asked, perplexed. "The doorway is much too small, and look, there's no broken glass anywhere."

"This is most puzzling," said Sersha. "We need to talk to the fairies that worked on fixing it after we returned from rescuing Sarah and the girls. Remember, it short circuited or something. The technician who worked on it said there were archives. Maybe that will tell us something. How the sphere works, what its capabilities are; I don't even know if Mother knows all its functions. Valian, can you go to the kitchen and fetch her?"

Valian nodded and went for the door.

"I'll go with you," said Henry.

As they left the room, Haley sat in one of the chairs, silent for a few minutes. She looked over at Sersha.

"Has anything like this ever happened before?" she asked.

"No."

"How old are you?" Haley asked.

"I don't know," Sersha answered.

"You don't know?"

"Time is different here. I wouldn't begin to guess what it would be in human years."

Haley gazed at her in wonder.

"You are amazing," she said. "You don't know how old you are, and you don't care. In my world, it's a big deal."

"Why?" Sersha asked.

"Well, certain things happen at different ages which people look forward to, like at five or six years old you get to go to school, and at fourteen or fifteen you get to go to high school. Then, at eighteen, you can vote, and at twenty-one, you are of age and free to go out and begin your own life without having to have permission."

Sersha looked at Haley curiously.

"What about love? When are you allowed to love?"

Haley gave her a surprised look.

"We love from the day we are born. You don't have to be a certain age, and it's not something that has to be allowed, it's a natural function, emotion everyone is born with."

"I have never experienced that kind of love," said Sersha in a faraway voice. "I have had what you might say, pangs on occasion, but since I removed my given gem, I have felt a welling up in my heart. It feels good and yet, at the same time, is an anxious feeling. I don't understand it."

"You will, in time," Haley said, smiling. "And who do you feel this pang for?"

Sersha blushed, which pleased Haley, but she didn't answer the question.

"You're coming around," Haley said with a chuckle.

Sersha smiled.

Suddenly, Valian and Henry burst into the room.

"Mother is missing!" Valian said, trying to catch his breath.

Sersha and Haley stood, shocked at the news.

"Oh, my gosh, what is happening?" Sersha cried, near tears.

"I don't know," said Valian, "but we must find her and quickly. If word gets out about this, we'll have a panic on our hands."

"Tell me what happened?" Haley asked anxiously.

"We went to the kitchen," Valian began. "The brownies were doing dishes, and we asked where Mother was, and they said she hadn't been there. Then we ran to her bedroom, but it was empty. We found this lying in the hall by the dining room." He held out his hand. "It's a given gem, and it's not mother's."

Sersha put her hand to her mouth.

Valian put his hand on her shoulder. "We'll check the sacred scrolls."

Haley gave him a questioning look.

"A record is kept of every gem given out by the Lords and Ladies of the realm," he explained. "Each gem has special markings etched in the back, not visible to the naked eye."

He walked over to the empty wood brace. In the wall behind it was a small door. He put in his hand and withdrew what looked like a magnifying glass.

"That's a magnifying glass," said Haley.

"Not just any old magnifying glass," said Valian. "This is special. It can see what is hidden," he said, turning around with a grin.

He held the gem up to the magnifying glass and gazed into it.

"There it is. Have a look," he said, handing it to Haley.

Everyone took turns looking into the glass. Haley saw what looked like tiny symbols.

"What is it?" she asked.

"Let's get the scrolls," said Valian.

They left the sacred chamber and arrived at the library moments later.

"You have a library?" Haley asked in amazement.

"Yes," Sersha answered. "The books and materials in here are ancient. They go back to the beginning, I think."

"To the beginning of what?" Henry asked.

"The beginning of time; the beginning of fairies I guess."

Haley was intrigued. She loved history.

"Oh, I'd love to have a look," she said excitedly.

"No time for that my sweet," said Valian, turning around with a dusty old scroll the size of a roll of postage stamps.

"I think this is the one," he said, unrolling it out across a nearby table.

"My goodness, that's small," said Haley, holding down one end of the scroll with her finger.

Valian scanned the length of the scroll looking for a match.

"Here it is," he said, pointing.

Sure enough, the symbols matched, and next to the symbol was the name Finn.

"Finn!" said Valian, stunned. "I never would have guessed . . . well, now we know there are at least four behind what's been happening."

"Four?" Henry asked.

"Yes, the two guardians in charge of protecting the sphere, Thorp and Dinora, and also Reed and Finn."

"Dinora, is that a female?" Haley asked.

"Yes," said Sersha. "She is a strong warrior. She will be a challenge to find."

"Okay, what do they look like?" Haley asked.

"They both have bronze skin and jet-blue eyes," said Sersha. "We'll take you to the royal artists. Their job is to sketch every fairy in the land. Every fairy has to have a portrait in their home for identification."

"Wow! Like an ID card or driver's license," said Henry.

"Follow me," said Valian.

The foursome left the library. *"I'm going to have to visit here again soon,"* Haley thought to herself.

They walked through the now deserted dining hall, down a corridor to the door of a veranda. The door was ajar, and there were puddles of water on the floor.

"Look," said Sersha, pointing at a torn piece of red silk lying on the floor next to the door. She picked it up and examined it.

"This is Mother's!" she exclaimed. "She was wearing a red silk gown today. She must have been taken as she walked through the dining hall on her way to the kitchen! They have a lot of nerve to kidnap a queen, and in broad daylight!" she said, slamming her fist on the wall.

Valian smiled at his sister. "Enjoying your new emotions?" he asked, grinning.

"As a matter of fact, I am," she answered, grinning at the others. "Let's go; now I'm mad!"

Sersha led the way, taking flight through the drizzling rain, heading east.

A few minutes later they landed just past the forest floor in a large well groomed yard. The property was enclosed by a three foot rock wall with a wrought iron gate. A sign post stood near the entrance that read:

Whispering Pines Sanctuary.

It was well named as the yard had dozens of mature pine trees, loaded with cones.

A cobblestone path led to the double front doors of a beautiful stone house. It was a single story with several chimneys. Blue smoke rose from them, disappearing quickly in the rain.

Valian opened the gate, and as they entered the grounds, they could hear the tinkling of dozens of wind chimes hanging from the long covered deck eves.

The porch ran the length of the house and had comfy tables and chairs placed neatly in small groups. It reminded Haley of walking through a furniture store, with its sofas and chairs set up like small rooms.

There were many potted plants, lanterns, and candles as well, giving it a real homey feel.

As soon as they stepped onto the deck, the wind chimes all stopped simultaneously.

"Just like a doorbell, huh?" Haley said to Henry.

Henry grinned.

Before Valian could knock, the double doors opened.

"Prince Valian! How wonderful it is to see you!" said an older male fairy.

Haley liked this fairy at once. He had long gray hair pulled back into a ponytail with a very large bald spot on the top of his head. He wore dark purple, square spectacles on the end of his nose, and had a sparkle in his deep blue eyes.

His magnificent silver-gold wings fanned themselves slowly as he shook Valian's hand.

"I heard you come up the walk," he smiled as little dimples appeared on his rosy cheeks.

"Jules," said Valian, with a small bow, "I would like you to meet two very dear friends of mine. This is Henry . . . "

Jules shook Henry's hand vigorously.

"And this is his sister Haley, my betrothed."

"Well, well, how do you do, milady," he said, enthusiastically shaking her hand. "Julius Caesar at your service."

"Julius Caesar?" the twins echoed.

"There was a Julius Caesar in our history!" Henry exclaimed.

"Yes, well, he was a funny little man . . . "

"Welcome, princess," he said to Sersha, interrupting himself.

"What was I saying? Oh yes, he was a bit strange and eccentric . . . I never really liked him much. Had a bit of a jealous streak in him. He was always trying to compete with me. Hated the fact that our family was so popular with the . . . what do you call it . . . high society?"

He turned, leading them through a posh living room with several entertainment areas separated by large silk screens. Plush couches, chairs, chaise lounges, and, of all things, beautifully embroidered hammocks hung around the room. The large windows were adorned with thick draperies, and blue logs crackled in the fireplace.

"Anyway, he became involved in politics, stole my name, and was placed in charge of the army of the day. Oh well, what's in a name, right?" he chuckled.

"You're the real Julius Caesar? That's incredible!" said Haley in awe.

"Yes, well, that's ancient history. Julius is long gone, and I'm still here, living out my days in peace and quiet. So, . . . what is the reason for this pleasant visit?" he asked, turning to Valian.

"I thought you might show Henry and Haley your work," Valian answered sheepishly.

"Wonderful! I haven't had many visitors lately. Seems the fairies are too busy with the hustle and bustle to appreciate the arts. This way," he said, leading them through covered gardens with many exotic plants and varieties of flowers.

Haley drank it all in.

There were many spouting fountains, small pools covered in lily pads, and several waterfalls, their rocks blanketed with creeping ivy. Upon closer inspection, she saw beautiful, brightly colored fish swimming lazily, and every so often, the splash of a tail disturbed the smooth surface.

"Oh, look," she said. "Aren't they beautiful?"

Julius turned.

"Bocan fish," he said. "I haven't seen them for years. They just turned up."

"What do you mean turned up?" Henry asked.

"My pools are set up with underground passages that lead out of the grounds. I don't know how far they go, but Bocan fish are rumored to live out far beyond the realm, even venturing as far as the Spicewood realm. Why they turned up here, I can't say."

"Bocan fish, huh," said Valian. "I wonder. Have you seen Tibit?"

"As a matter of fact, just this morning."

"Who's Tibit?" Haley asked.

"He is the leader of the Bocan's," Julius replied. "He's a friendly chap but a bit paranoid I think. He was mumbling something about ferocious stalk beasts scattering the schools."

"Bulwarks," said Sersha. "Maybe he knows something about what happened to them. Is he here?"

"I haven't seen him since this morning."

Valian leaned over one of the pools.

"Excuse me," said Valian.

Several of the fish stopped to look up at him.

"Excuse me, might I have a word with you?"

One of the fish rose slowly to the surface and poked its head out of the water.

"Would Tibet be among you?"

The fish gave Valian a half-hearted smile.

"No, haven't seen him," it replied in a watery gurgle.

Haley gasped.

"Oh, my gosh, he's huge!"

"And he can talk," Henry added, his eyes wide.

"Did you happen to be there when the stalk beasts attacked the Bocan pond?" Valian asked.

"No, I wasn't," said the fish in a loud voice, disappearing back into the water.

"Well, that was rude," said Haley. "What's happening to all these water creatures?"

"I haven't the foggiest," said Julius. "It seems like perhaps dark forces are at work here. Come, follow me to the gallery."

The group followed Julius through a vine-covered arbor plastered with delicate orange flowers and through the adjacent open stone courtyard.

Haley had to stop and look around. There were many wall-mounted water features surrounded by lush green plants. Large tropical trees with huge leaves surrounded another pond lined with tall reeds, water lilies, and cattails.

A large gargoyle spat a long stream of water into the center of the pond, and several loungers sat empty in the light rain.

Julius directed them ahead to the next building and into a long rectangular room. It had a glass roof that lit up the rows and rows of easels displaying portraits of dozens of fairies. Some were painted and some were drawn in charcoal, others in pen and ink.

"Wow," said Haley softly. "These are incredible. Look at the detail," she added.

Julius stood there and smiled.

"Not bad if I do say so myself."

"Did you do all these?" she asked.

"Many," said Julius, "but not all. The other artists are very talented."

"Where are the other artists?" she asked.

"They are on retreat in the mountains of the Tempest region in the Palm realm."

"With such a beautiful place as this, how could anyone need a retreat from it?" Haley asked in awe.

"Oh, this sanctuary is fitting for doing portraits," said Julius, "but occasionally, they need to get away to be inspired by nature's beauty."

Haley walked down the rows, examining the displays.

"Are these all you have?" she asked.

"No, would you care to see the archives?"

"Yes, please," she answered.

Julius walked to the end of the room and opened the door to a room that seemed endless, with racks and racks filled with portraits. It was like a library.

"I thought these were all supposed to be in fairy homes," said Haley.

"They are," Julius replied. "These are old and outdated. Fairies grow older and change, similar to humans."

"Oh, I get it," said Haley. "Duh!"

Henry chuckled.

Valian led the group down the dusty isle, stopped midway, and began pulling out portraits until he found what he was looking for.

"This is Thorp," he said, handing the portrait to Haley.

Thorp was a splendid-looking fairy with bronze skin, jet-blue eyes, and long, wavy brown hair. He was husky and short, from what she could tell, and quite muscular. He wore golden hoop earrings in both ears and had a thin brown mustache, and a small goatee.

"I've never seen a fairy with facial hair," she commented.

"He is not of the Manwan race," Valian replied. "Manwans cannot grow facial hair."

He moved further up the aisle and retrieved two more portraits. Haley handed Thorp's portrait to Henry as Valian handed her the next one.

"That is Dinora."

Haley let out a small gasp. "Wow," she said.

Staring up at her was the angriest-looking fairy she'd ever seen. Dinora was also bronze skinned with the same jet blue eyes as Thorp's. Her eyebrows were tilted at such an angle as to make her look like she was glaring at the artist.

"She looks really mad," she said, looking up at Valian.

"No, that is her normal face," said Valian.

Haley shook her head. Dinora looked quite a bit taller than her cousin and was just as muscular, and she could see just a hint of hair above Dinora's lip.

"I wouldn't want to run into her in a dark alley," said Henry, looking over Haley's shoulder.

Haley giggled and rolled her eyes.

"And this is Finn," said Valian.

Finn looked nothing like the other two. He looked small in stature, had pale green eyes, almost yellow, and a rather flat nose. He wore a sheepish grin for this picture.

"How old are these, Julius?" Haley asked, turning toward him.

"Please, call me Jules. I'd say roughly twenty-five of your years."

"So, you don't think there has been much change?"

"Not likely," he replied. "What's your interest in these three?" Julius asked.

"Oh . . . I just wanted to show some of the four-hundred-tenth academy cadets. One of my most successful sessions . . . " Valian lied, "since Henry and Haley are going to become guardians one day soon, I hope."

Haley raised an eyebrow at him with a smile on her face. It seemed lying was not difficult for him, except he didn't quite have the knack for it. There was a slight quiver in his voice, and he kept swallowing.

"Well, thank you for the tour," Valian said, changing the subject. "I wish to show my betrothed everything Roan and the Woodland realm have to offer."

"It's a good thing you're starting now," said Julius. "It'll take you three years to show her everything."

"Ha, ha, yes indeed," said Valian. "Shall we go?" he asked, ushering Haley back toward the rectangular room.

"Shall I see you out?" Julius asked.

"Not at all," Valian answered. "I am sure we can find our way. Thank you again for your time, Jules."

"It was nice to meet you, Jules," Haley called over her shoulder.

"My pleasure," Julius called back as they stepped into the open courtyard.

"This place is just wondrous," Haley was saying, as they took flight. "Are there many places like this?"

"Thousands, I suppose," Valian answered, "maybe tens of thousands."

"You know what I just realized?" said Haley, "We never changed size. That whole place was as tiny as Roan!"

She took a deep, satisfied breath as they flew hand in hand back toward the palace.

Chapter Seven

VIOLET'S HORROR

Violet sat at the window of her cottage, daydreaming while she ate a late lunch. Out of the corner of her eye she saw movement and looked up just in time to see Valian, Haley, Henry, and Sersha fly through the canopy, quickly disappearing in the leaves.

She threw her lunch into the sink and began her usual pacing. She had become nervous lately, wondering as everyone else what was happening to the Woodland realm and its creatures, and about how angry Maximillion would be when he found out about Haley and Valian's betrothal.

"Well, it was bound to happen," she said to herself. "After all, they are not married yet and won't be for three years. I've got plenty of time. Since I've already taken the potion, one look at me, and he'll drop that human like a hot rock." She grinned to herself. "As a matter of fact, there's no time like the present."

She shot out of her doorway, hot on Valian's trail. As the castle came into view the courtyard was empty. The palace doors were wide open as the guardians didn't come on duty until well after dark, and fairies were free to come and go until then, although there were still certain areas within the castle heavily guarded. She had never seen the interior except for the great dining room and only on special occasions and, of course, the little excursion to Haley's room. She was not part of the Lord's and Lady's court.

She was taking a risk in coming here, though, since she didn't show up for her shift at the infirmary. She didn't want to run into anyone she worked with.

She walked into the dining room. There were only a few fairies sitting at a table together, talking, and they didn't notice she had come in. Her curiosity got the better of her, and she turned down the hallway the queen usually entered from.

She stopped abruptly as she spotted a female guardian headed in her direction. The guardian held up her hand as she approached.

"This is a restricted area," the guardian said, firmly. "Do you have a pass?"

"No, I'm sorry, I was just hoping to have a word with the prince," Violet stammered.

"The prince has not returned," said the guardian, giving Violet an odd look. She took out a small scroll and unrolled it. "His itinerary says he is probably arriving at Mathilda's right about now." The scroll rolled itself up with a snap.

"Thank you," said Violet, turning back toward the dining room.

The guardian watched her with a raised eyebrow, shook her head and went back the way she came.

Violet sped towards Mathilda's, excitement growing on her face, ready to steal Valian's affections.

"I can't wait to see the look on that human's face," she giggled.

She glided in softly, landing across the street from Mathilda's food court, which was empty because of the rain. She walked swiftly across the street. The low rumble of thunder echoed through the outskirts.

She peeked through one of the windows and saw the happy couple sitting in the back with Sersha and Henry and about a dozen other guardians. The section was roped off to keep other patrons from intruding.

"I suppose they're having another meeting about the stupid bulwarks," she mumbled to herself.

Quietly she let herself inside and walked up to the high counter.

"May I help you?"

Violet looked at the old crone, hunched over with straggly white hair and a face full of warts.

"Yes," she answered, holding her head high.

"I need to have a word with Prince Valian."

The crone opened her mouth to respond, but Violet didn't give her a chance.

"It is urgent business from Queen Lilia," she lied.

The crone gave her a nod. "Wait here," she said, walking around the counter and over to the roped-off section.

She went up to Valian, bent over and whispered to him. Valian stood at once, looking past the crone to where Violet stood. He bent down and said something to the others, then turned toward her.

Haley looked toward the counter and her face went red and her mouth hung open.

It was just the reaction Violet hoped for. She drew in a deep breath, puffed her chest and put on her best innocent smile, fanning her wings in the most provocative way as her heart hammered in her chest.

"Violet?" he said as he stood in front of her.

"Prince Valian," she said sweetly, batting her eyes. "How are you feeling?"

He took her by the arm.

"Come with me," he said, leading her toward an empty, smaller dining room.

Violet looked over her shoulder with an evil, triumphant sneer at Haley, as Haley just sat there frozen and white-faced.

Valian steered her into the far corner of the room, and they sat across from each other at one of the tables.

"Well?" he asked.

Violet batted her eyes again and fanned her wings slowly. She gave him the most seductive look she knew how.

"Prince Valian, I am worried about you," she said coyly.

Valian raised his eyebrows as if to ask, "Well?"

Violet went on.

"I am worried that you're moving too fast and taking on too much since your injury. I . . . "

"What about the queen?" he asked. "You said you were here on business from the queen."

Violet sat quietly for a moment.

"What about the queen?" he asked again, his voice raising an octave. "Has she sent a message?"

"Oh, that," she giggled. "I just said that to get you alone for a moment," she answered, beaming at him.

"What?" Valian demanded, his voice loud and booming.

Violet's face went ashen.

"How dare you!" he said, now yelling. "How dare you come here and lie to me!"

His voice quickly got the attention of the guardians in the other room, and they came bursting through the door, swords drawn. Valian paid no attention to them.

"How dare you!" he yelled again.

The anger had clearly risen in him as his face grew rosy. Little beads of sweat began to form on his upper lip and his ears grew red.

"You come here for what reason I can only guess! Perhaps to come between me and my betrothed! You are not worthy to call yourself a loyal citizen! I shall banish . . . "

At that moment, Haley gently laid her hand on Valian's arm.

Violet sat there trembling in her seat. Her face was white, and her wings were tucked behind her back.

Looking down at the pitiful sight in front of her, Haley felt sorry for her. She looked up into Valian's pale blue eyes.

"Darling, have mercy on her."

Valian looked at Haley, and his face softened.

"She doesn't know any better," she continued. "She obviously has feelings for you. What would any girl do in her shoes?" she smiled lovingly at him.

"You are most gracious, my sweet," Valian said softly.

"Let her go," said Haley.

Violet gained some of her composure, nodding her head at Haley's suggestion but she herself began to turn red with anger and cast an evil look at Haley.

"You are free to go," said Valian, turning toward the door.

"What?" Haley exclaimed, startled.

Valian turned back and looked at Violet. Her long beautiful blonde hair began to change color to a dark, purple-gray color.

Violet looked at them with a questioning look.

"Your hair," Haley stammered.

Violet frowned and grasped a lock of her hair, brought it before her eyes, and let out a shriek.

Haley took a step backward.

"Your arms and face . . ."

Violet looked down at her arms. Small black blotches had begun to form. She felt her face as the black blotches turned into raised welts, and suddenly, out of her forehead sprang two tentacles that looked like the feelers you would see on a snail.

Haley let out a squeal and stifled a laugh as she watched the feelers thrash around wildly. They were slimy and left little trails on Violet's forehead as they felt their way around.

Violet felt a drop of ooze fall on her nose. She wiped it on the back of her hand, looked at it, and let out another shriek. She stood abruptly, knocking over her chair, trembling. Glaring at Haley, she stammered. "This isn't over . . . not by a long shot!"

She turned and tore out of the room, shrieking as she went.

Everyone looked at each other, stunned.

Haley went over to the window, Valian behind her. They watched Violet stumble through the door as she left the building. She tore through the tables, turned, and looked back. She had a terrified look on her face, but the rage was what stood out for Haley. Violet snapped her wings furiously and shot over the trees and out of sight.

"What happened to her?" she asked, turning to Valian.

"My guess is that she was trying to use magic. Not fairy magic but perhaps witches' magic."

"Witches' magic?"

"She must be in cahoots with someone, but I don't have a clue as to who it could be. She sure was ticked off, though, wasn't she?" said Valian, chuckling.

Haley flashed him a half-hearted smile.

"It would have been really funny if it hadn't been so scary. Whatever spell she tried to use must have backfired."

"Backfired is putting it mildly," said Valian. "She obviously totally screwed it up. You don't ever try to mess with another species' magic, it's taboo."

"As it should be," said Haley. "Could she get into trouble for that?"

"Yes, but I think she's had punishment enough, don't you?"

"Oh, my goodness did you see those feelers, how they just popped out of her head?" Haley giggled.

"I wonder what she was trying to do," he laughed.

"I should think probably a love potion," Haley answered.

Valian looked at her curiously.

"Well, you said it yourself. She's been trying to come between us. I could see that the first moment I laid eyes on her. Her holding your hand in the infirmary and the look on her face, I knew then she was going to be a problem."

"You know who my heart belongs to," he said, looking into her eyes.

He put his hands around her head and softly caressed her hair.

"I love you."

"Ahem."

Valian turned. He had forgotten Sersha, Henry, and the other guardians were in the room. They were all looking in different directions, pretending to be interested in a particular spot on the ceiling or the chairs and such.

Valian smiled.

"Sorry, shall we get back to the meeting?" he said, blushing slightly.

He stopped at the counter and told Mathilda not to allow any more interruptions as they returned to the roped-off area.

They decided to split into teams. Haley and Valian would take two guardians and head for the islands while Sersha and Henry would take two and go back to the other side, just in case, to make sure there wasn't anything going on there.

"When shall we leave?" Haley asked.

"The sooner, the better," Sersha answered, with a look of sheer determination on her face. "Whoever took Mother and the sphere . . . they're gonna pay for what they have done."

Haley smiled and gave Sersha a pat on the shoulder.

"We need to prepare," said Valian. "We'll need supplies, and Henry, we're gonna need that map to lay out our route. I'm pretty sure which way to go, but as I said before, I don't recognize the lay of the land there. We'll get our swords, bow and arrows, and something special . . . Cupid's arrows."

"Cupid, are you kidding me?" Henry asked, in surprise. "Cupid is real? I can't believe it!"

"Believe it," Sersha smiled.

"Alright, so what happens when you shoot Cupid's arrow at someone? Do they fall in love?" he asked.

"Sometimes," Sersha answered. "The effects are a little different for each individual. It's hard for me to explain; you'll have to see for yourself."

The group decided to stay at Mathilda's for dinner. Since the queen was gone from the palace, it wouldn't seem unusual for them to be absent.

Valian, on the other hand, was trying to figure out what to tell the Lords and Ladies of the royal court about a missing queen.

Haley suggested he tell them she went on a vacation and that they would be joining her. They all agreed it was a good idea but decided to call it a retreat since no one had ever heard of the term vacation.

They hurried through dinner and headed back to the palace to get the supplies organized.

Henry and Sersha went to the kitchen to get food, mostly dried fruits, nuts, bread, and Vimsom fruit.

Haley had eaten Vimsom once before. It was called Vimsom fruit, but it was actually a refreshing and filling vegetable shaped like an octopus, and you could only eat the arms.

Valian sent out messengers to spread the word of the meeting before breakfast, and the guardians who attended the meeting at Mathilda's gathered in the blue room with the foursome to go over final plans. They all enjoyed large steins of ember potion.

Valian chose the four guardians that would go with the parties, and the rest were instructed to keep things under control in Roan, especially any talk or rumors that might crop up about the royal family being on retreat.

After everyone received their assignments, the guardians were dismissed. Valian, Haley, Sersha, and Henry sat close together, just like a family, giving each other words of encouragement and just enjoying each other's company.

"Make sure to check on Mom and Dad when you're back there," said Haley anxiously. "I know Estelle put a spell on them, but it would be good to see they're alright."

"I will," said Henry. "We'll fly up to their window and peek in on them, and you two, you be careful and keep your minds on business," he added with a grin.

Valian turned red, and Haley smiled and rolled her eyes.

"You know you're getting pretty good at that," said Henry, looking at Valian.

"Good at what?" he asked.

"At being embarrassed."

Valian turned even redder, as did the points of his ears.

"Don't you worry about it," said Haley, smiling at the prince. "I think it makes you look gallant."

"Well, thank you, my sweet," said Valian, as he kissed her hand and gave Henry the eye.

Haley looked over and saw Sersha was starting to nod off.

"Come on you guys, we need to get to bed."

Everyone went to their rooms and fell asleep as soon as their heads hit the pillow. No one dreamed that night, and they slept more deeply than they ever had before.

Haley was suddenly jerked out of a sound sleep. She thought she heard a loud bang and sat up, looking around. *"I must have dreamt it,"* she thought to herself. All was quiet, and the room was bright with sunshine.

"Oh, my gosh, I've overslept!" she said aloud.

She heard a banging on her door, and she jumped out of bed and ran to the door.

"Yes?" she called out.

It was Henry.

"Get up! We've all overslept! I had to wake Valian and Sersha. They're waking up the guardians. The dining room is full and everyone is waiting for us. They've already had breakfast!"

"Oh, my goodness!" she answered, running for a fresh gown. "I'll be there as fast as I can!"

She hurriedly dressed and flew out the door, running down the hall to the dining room.

When she arrived, Valian, Sersha, Henry, and the rest of the party had just arrived. She took her seat by the others as Valian stood to address the Lords and Ladies of the royal court.

"My apologies, everyone; I'm sorry to have kept you waiting. I think we overdid it with the ember potion last night."

The room responded with laughter.

"I've gathered you all here to let you know that Haley, myself, Sersha, and Henry are going on a retreat for a while."

There were smiles and nods from the audience as he continued.

"Queen Lilia has also decided to take a retreat and has already left. We'll be joining her later today."

Valian swallowed, and Haley could see his ears getting pink.

"I have put the guardians in charge of seeing to it that day-to-day activities run smoothly and order is kept. If any concerns come up you will report to them. It's been quite some time since we've been able to get away and relax and enjoy the countryside. We won't be gone long, so don't get too comfortable with the head of the table," he said, grinning at the guardians.

The assembly laughed again.

"Here, Here!" yelled someone in the crowd as everyone clapped.

"That will be all then," he said, turning toward Sersha and the twins.

"Fair thee well," yelled several fairies as the group left for the blue room.

The brownies came in and served them a private breakfast. After the brownies had gone, Valian looked at the others.

"When we've finished eating, let's all freshen up and meet on the terrace."

Haley showered and grabbed her knapsack. She tied it around her waist and met the others on the terrace.

It was a beautiful day. The sun was shining, the rain and storms forgotten.

The twins were really excited about embarking on a new adventure. Even Valian and Sersha seemed eager.

The guardians joined them moments later. They were all armed and also carried knapsacks similar to Haley's.

Sersha handed Haley and Henry a small drawstring bag.

"Here, attach these to your knapsacks."

"What is it?" Henry asked.

"Armor, it's traditional guardian attire. I know you're not guardians yet, but you may need these clothes. You each have a dragon skin vest and tunic."

"I didn't have time to give them to you this morning," she continued, "and I didn't want you wearing them at breakfast. We don't want to raise suspicion and have the whole of the city thinking we were going into battle."

"Right," said Henry, "Gotcha."

"Well, this is it, you guys," said Sersha. "We'll fly out just past the outskirts then we'll split up."

The group leaped from the terrace and glided over the treetops.

Minutes later, they landed just above the outskirts at the top of the canyon overlooking the small community.

Hilda and Estelle were on the dirt path, waiting for them.

"Right on time," said Hilda with a smile.

After greetings were over, Hilda and Estelle inspected everyone to be sure gear was in order and wings were in tip-top shape. Satisfied, Hilda pulled two blue stones from her pocket. They were the size of a small plum and were perfectly round and smooth, like large marbles.

"These stones have been bewitched," she said. "If either team is in trouble, rap it against the ground three times. The other team's stone will glow and give off a strong shock. It will also show your location."

She handed a stone to Valian and one to Henry.

"Go, find your mother. Fair thee well," she said, turning to Henry and Sersha, giving them hugs.

"Good luck to you. I hope you find everything is well on the other side. Come back with some good news."

Haley turned to Henry and Sersha and gave them both a big hug.

"I love you guys . . . be safe."

She watched them take flight and quickly vanish into the trees. She was feeling anxious and a little scared, her brother going off without her. They had never been apart before and she was worried.

Valian was watching her and put his hand on her wing, turning her toward him.

"They'll be fine, my sweet. Henry is quite capable. I've seen him in battle, and I can assure you he is strong and able, and he's in good company."

"Thank you," Haley smiled. "I needed that, and I'm glad you are reading my expressions so well."

"Let's get going," he smiled back.

They took flight, heading south, making good time. The wind was at their backs and made flying easier. After several hours, they stopped to rest on the edge of dark wood and snacked on some Vimsom fruit.

"We should probably change size before we go on," said Valian. "We'll be harder to spot if we're smaller."

"That's a good idea," Haley agreed.

With a snap of spark, they shrank and took flight, zipping into the canopy.

Chapter 8

JOURNEY INTO THE UNKNOWN

Henry, Sersha, and their guardians flew over the tree tops, heading for the nearest portal. Henry turned for one last glimpse of his sister. His heart was heavy and he had a serious look on his face. Sersha grabbed his hand.

He turned to her, surprised.

"Don't worry about them," she said. "Valian is the best in the land. If anyone can protect her, he can," she smiled.

He smiled back. His serious face disappeared and was replaced with pleasure. He quickly let go of Sersha's hand and looked ahead, his cheeks turning pink.

Sersha smiled to herself as she scanned ahead, watching for the familiar glittering tower.

"Where are we headed?" Henry yelled out.

"There is a tower just ahead!" she replied.

They dove over the side of a cliff, surrounded by a glen filled with daisies. Next to the base of the cliff was a glittering tower of sparkle, swirling slowly. It was a whirlwind full of glittering, colorful particles. Henry was familiar with these towers, having fallen into one with Haley on the other side when they first discovered the land of Wisen.

They swooped down to the bottom and landed in front of the entrance to a cave.

"How come I can see the towers on this side but not on the other side?" Henry asked.

"They're charmed," Sersha answered. "We can't have humans able to see them and have them entering our world. There would be nothing but trouble having those who are not of good heart entering and wreaking havoc, taking our gems back to their side. Your world as you know it would be destroyed by greed and corruption. The hearts of men can be swayed easily by the promise of wealth and power, but I'm sure you already know that."

"Yeah," said Henry, shaking his head. "What a bummer, huh?"

Sersha gave him a reassuring smile and looked at the guardians.

"I'm sorry," she said suddenly. "I never introduced you! Henry, this is Troy and Theodore. They have been with us for half a century. They were in the last graduating class."

Henry held his hand in the air.

"Give me five," he said.

Troy and Theodore gave him a strange look and turned to Sersha.

She had seen behavior such as this before while observing humans through the sphere. She smiled and gave Henry a high five.

"It's like a hand shake," she said, laughing at Troy and Theodore as they awkwardly tried giving each other a high five. Their attempts resulted in slaps in the face.

Henry burst out laughing and showed them how to do it right.

"Okay," said Sersha, "we're gonna have to change size. This portal comes out right in the middle of a thorn bush, and we don't want to get all tangled up in that."

Everyone changed with a snap as Sersha led the way. One by one, they stepped into the tower and disappeared.

It was just as Henry remembered it. The group tumbled amongst the swirling waves of glitter as if in slow motion. It was bright and shining, reminding Henry of a roller coaster ride.

The opening at the other end grew larger and larger, and soon, they popped out like corks from a champagne bottle right into the bush. Henry had to veer left to avoid a giant thorn, just missing it by a hair.

They were at the top of a large bluff. It was pitch dark out, which made it difficult for Henry to figure out where they were.

"Alright, Henry, this is your territory," said Sersha.

He scanned the horizon, looking for any familiar landmark. Way off in the distance he saw the faint glow of a light.

"Let's head for that light," he said, motioning to the others.

They flew quietly, taking it nice and slow. It was a warm summer night. The humidity was high, making Henry perspire a bit. Sersha flew alongside him, her eyes sharp and focused.

The crickets chirped loudly as they flew across a large, empty field. As the light drew nearer, Henry had the feeling he knew where he was. As they approached the top of a wooded hill, he knew instantly. They were at the Seers' property.

They landed in the trees and looked down at a magnificent house. It had a triple -tiered yard with a mountain stream running through it. An old carousel sat abandoned next to the house. Every window was lit up, and the sound of voices, music, and laughter were quickly muted by the surrounding hills.

They sat quietly and watched as a door opened, and a man with a torch came out laughing, followed by at least twenty people.

The man descended the first tier, lighting other torches along the path as he went.

The flickering of the flames revealed a swimming pool, patios, and flowerbeds. The people broke off in small groups, taking seats on lounge chairs, with some going to the pool for a dip.

"They're having a party," Henry whispered to Sersha. "This is Ike's house."

Sersha nodded.

"I remember," she said.

Henry looked at her questioningly.

She quickly told him about their experience with Ike when he was a teen. How he entered Wisen and how he was able to build this house and become very wealthy.

"He had a pure heart . . . once," she said sadly.

The music was turned up a notch, and couples began to dance and talk loudly. Drink glasses were refilled, and laughter was abundant.

Troy and Theodore watched, wide eyed as two girls disrobed, displaying tanned skin and tiny bikinis. They looked at each other as if appalled, then turned back to the swimmers.

"Interesting," said Troy.

"Very," Theodore added.

Henry and Sersha smiled at each other.

"You'd think they'd never seen a girl in a swimsuit," Henry chuckled, softly.

"They haven't," Sersha replied.

Henry gave her a look of surprise and glanced over at the guardians, who were entranced by the scene in front of them.

"Come on," said Henry, "let's get a closer look."

The guardians eagerly followed Henry and Sersha as they flew around the back side of the house to a weeping willow that grew on the edge of the grounds next to the pool and patio.

They were well hidden in the long willow branches and had a bird's eye view. They had a clear view of Ike as he walked around with a drink in his hand, talking loudly and boasting about his new yacht.

Half a dozen girls surrounded him, cooing over him, each one trying to gain his attention. Several of them were trying to coax him to the pool.

He acted pompously, his nose in the air with a stupid smirk on his face. He pretended to give in as he put his drink down on one of the umbrella-covered tables and proceeded to remove his polo shirt.

He was faced directly in front of the willow as he pulled the shirt over his head.

Sersha gasped.

Ike stopped suddenly and stood still for a moment as if listening.

Sersha covered her mouth. Henry looked at her. Half concerned that she may blow their cover, and half concerned she was afraid, though she'd never shown fear in front of him before. Who knew what she was capable of now that she wasn't wearing her given gem?

He mouthed the words, "What is it?"

She pointed at her own chest, tapping it, and pointed at Ike.

Henry looked and knew at once what her concern was. In the middle of Ike's chest was an obsidian stone, hanging from a chain. He knew that obsidian was bad, but he didn't know why. No one had ever explained the properties of obsidian to him, but the few times it was mentioned, Valian would spit.

The group watched quietly, each one of them on edge, ready to bolt from their hiding spots in a split second at any sign they'd been discovered.

Ike tossed his shirt onto the chair next to him and stood quite still. He slowly turned his head, studying the darkness as if he knew he was being watched. He stood there several minutes, then shrugged his shoulders and let the girls steer him to the pool.

"Whew, that was close," whispered Henry, relaxing a little.

He looked over at Sersha. She was all clenched up and tense, not moving a muscle. He reached over, grabbing her arm, startling her so that she almost toppled off her branch.

"Sorry, relax a little," he whispered, rubbing her arm. "You okay?"

She nodded.

After a couple of hours of watching, one by one, people began leaving. Some went into the house, and others left in their cars until only Ike and one other man were left.

The two men talked quietly as they sat in front of an elaborate round fire pit made of decorated stone and filled with lava rock.

"I can't hear them," said Henry. "We need to get closer."

Sersha gave him a pleading look as if to say 'no.'

"It'll be alright," Henry whispered, taking her by the hand.

Quietly, they flitted from tree to tree and hovered over a twelve-foot potted Japanese maple. Its branches extended out over the fire pit by a couple of feet. They landed in the uppermost branches. They didn't have the best view, but they could hear perfectly.

" . . . the ex," Ike was saying. "If she thinks I'm gonna let her have my boys and take half of everything I own, she's got another think coming."

Sersha and Henry looked at each other, eyebrows raised, then back towards Ike.

"Yep," said the stranger, "I know exactly what you're talkin' about."

"You know, I've got half a mind to let her have half, now that I think about it," said Ike.

"What?" the stranger asked.

"Yeah," said Ike. "That witch! I'll offer her half and make it a final deal. She'll jump at it, thinking I'm being fair," he laughed coldly. "Listen, I know of a way to get as much money as I will ever need . . . " he said quietly, pausing. "I want to tell you something, but you have to swear on your soul you won't tell anybody else."

The stranger leaned forward, listening eagerly.

"You swear?" Ike asked, in a threatening voice.

The stranger jerked his head back slightly, looking at Ike apprehensively and nodding.

"I've kept this a secret for so long; I've just been dying to tell someone."

The stranger leaned even closer as Ike whispered.

When he finished, the stranger began to laugh. He laughed loudly, slapping his knee, as tears rolled down his cheeks.

Ike got mad, really mad. His face turned red as he stood up and began to pace; all the while, the stranger continued to laugh.

"I . . . I'll prove it to you!" he said, loudly.

The stranger stood.

"Okay, Ike," he said, laughing and clapping him on the shoulder. "You show me."

"Come with me," said Ike.

He walked up the tiers to the front of the house, down the paved driveway to a large, padlocked shed, and took a key from his pocket.

"No one's ever been in here except me," he said, unlocking the door.

He flipped on the light and walked inside, the stranger right behind him with a curious look on his face.

He walked over to a locked tool chest; the kind that sits on the floor, with dozens of drawers.

The foursome flew toward the shed and took cover in a bush just across from the doorway.

"You three stay here," Henry instructed and flitted from the bush to the top of the door before Sersha could protest.

He landed softly and peered inside.

Ike unlocked the tool chest and pulled out a small sunglass case. He opened it and carefully pulled out a chain bearing a diamond pendant.

Henry felt a slight vibration as Sersha landed beside him. He gave her an exasperated look for not staying put.

As they peered in together, Sersha's mouth dropped open at the sight of the diamond necklace dangling from Ike's finger.

Ike opened another drawer and pulled out a tightly rolled-up piece of parchment.

It was Henry's turn for his mouth to drop open.

He and Sersha gave each other a look that didn't need explanation. It was an utter shock.

"This gem . . . is the key to seeing portals into the fairy world," said Ike, like he was talking to a child.

"This map . . . marks three portals that have been sealed . . . however, if you put on this necklace, a dozen more portals are revealed," he said with a sneer. "Zeb Bonner wasn't very bright when he drew this map. Luckily, I was the one to discover its secrets," he finished proudly.

The stranger looked at the three Xs as Ike slipped the chain over his head.

Ike watched as the stranger's eyes grew wide, then he quickly took back the necklace.

The stranger's face lit up with excitement and greed.

"Now," Ike began. "Working together, you and I have an opportunity . . . if we're smart, to amass greater wealth than anyone on the planet. You and I will sneak in under cover of dark and collect gems beyond your wildest imagination."

The stranger nodded his head eagerly.

"Now I have your promise, not a word to anyone."

It wasn't a question but a warning.

"Yes, of course," the stranger answered impatiently. "When do we go?"

"Soon," Ike answered, smiling at the fact that he now had the stranger under his control with the promise of riches.

"Where'd you get this stuff?" the stranger asked.

"Someone from the fairy world stole it and brought it to me," he answered triumphantly. "The stupid fools never even missed it," he cackled to himself.

Henry turned to Sersha and motioned with his shoulder for her to follow him. They flew back to the bush to collect the others, then flew back to the top of the bluff overlooking Ike's house.

They all began whispering at once. Henry raised his hand for silence. "Ladies first."

"That necklace is Valian's given gem!" Sersha exclaimed.

"And that parchment," said Henry excitedly. "Haley and I found that map, remember?"

Sersha was all a fluster about how Ike got his hands on the map and necklace and the fact that someone stole it for him.

"It was probably Reed," she said. "He's the only one who had access to areas off limits to everyone else."

Henry nodded in agreement.

"Ike was right about one thing," he said.

"What's that?"

"I never did realize the map was missing."

Violet flew half hazard, not really watching where she was going and not caring. She was just livid. She was so angry tears streamed down her face. Not just angry at Haley, but angry at Valian, about the things he said and the way he treated her. He embarrassed her in front of that human.

"That *human!*" she cried out, clenching her teeth. "I'll make her pay! Dismissing me like a lovesick little imp! Acted as though she felt sorry for me and was doing me a favor by suggesting Valian let me go. Argh!"

She felt her face, moving her fingers slowly toward the protrusions coming from her forehead. New tears warmed her face as she flew. Suddenly, she came to an abrupt halt in midair.

"I'll go see Maximillion," she said to herself. "He'll be able to fix this mess, and together, we'll help each other get what we want."

Violet smiled to herself, which quickly turned to a frown as she felt her face again. She would have to stay out of sight for a few days until her "affliction" cleared up, hopefully.

She turned around and headed for her cottage.

It was beginning to get dark. The clouds in the sky began to turn that pretty pink and red color that was so prominent in the land of Wisen.

The rain had let up, and everything was dripping. The smell of smoke hung in the air as she quickly and silently weaved her way through the forest.

Violet arrived home just as the sun was shining its last rays before dipping below the horizon.

She entered her dark cottage, slammed the door, and stormed into her bathroom. She was afraid to light up the room and look in the mirror.

With a sigh, she waved her hand. The lantern gave off a soft glow as she slowly turned toward the mirror. Violet gasped, and a squeal escaped her lips. New tears of anger and embarrassment rolled down her cheeks. Dark patches covered her face and neck and the long feelers were grotesque and slimy, and she had a sudden urge for the smell of dirt.

She sobbed and half staggered to the flower pot in the kitchenette. She grabbed a handful of soil and put it up to her nose when she suddenly had the feeling she wasn't alone.

Violet turned slowly and gasped at the silhouette sitting in the chair. She couldn't tell who it was in the dark shadows of the room, but she could feel the anger emanating towards her.

The candelabra in the room suddenly came to life. The flickering light cast dancing shadows across Maximillion's face.

Maximillion began to laugh. It was a sinister, cold laugh.

Violet stood there silent and scared, her knees shaking.

"You didn't follow my instructions, did you?" he asked.

"I . . . I'm pretty sure I did," she answered.

"Tell me how you did it," said the sorcerer.

Violet explained exactly how she picked the toadstools, mixed them with the potion and how she drank the mixture.

A slight grin crossed Maximillion's face.

"Toadstools huh? Did I say toadstools?" he asked with a frown. "No, I said TOADSTOOL! And you waited too long."

"Huh?"

"Not only did you use more than one, but you let it wither away. Once you picked it, you were supposed to mix the *blood* of the toadstool with the potion, not the *entire* toadstool. Not only was it withered, but the blood had dried up, and you should have done it all within an hour's time."

Fresh tears began to well up in Violet's eyes.

Maximillion rolled his eyes and let out an exasperated sigh.

"You stupid child," he said, standing up and putting his hand inside his robes.

"How long will I be this way?" she sobbed.

"Unfortunately, without the proper antidote, the effects are permanent."

Violet continued to sob, covering her face.

Maximillion shook his head, slightly irritated.

"Here," he said, handing her what looked like an ordinary rock. "I figured you'd mess it up."

She looked up. As soon as she took her hands away from her face, the long feelers began to move across the streams of tears, soaking up all the moisture they could get. One of them latched onto the corner of her eye with a suction sound, making her shriek and yank at it, trying to get it off, but to no avail, it held fast. The tips of the feelers had minute little teeth like a leech and couldn't be forcibly removed. It stung her eye, making it water as the feeler intended. She looked at Maximillion.

"Please . . . please help me."

Maximillion gave her a pathetic smile. He was amused.

"Boil this rock in water for twenty minutes and then drink it," he commanded authoritatively.

Violet eagerly took the rock. It felt dirty like it was covered in a fine layer of grit. She got up and prepared a pot and put in the rock. As she waited for the water to boil, she began to pace.

Her other feeler found the corner of her other eye and she let out a shriek as her eyes began to water even more.

"Why are you helping me?" she asked, yanking at the feelers. "I haven't gotten anywhere with Haley yet."

It was her hope that Maximillion would believe she was really Haley's friend and that it was just a matter of time.

"You're no good to me in this condition," he said, motioning toward her face. "I do rather enjoy a good disfigurement from time to time. However, we're running out of time as Haley is already betrothed."

Violet stopped pacing and froze.

"I'm sorry, Maximillion," she begged. "It happened before I could even get near her. That little twit human is cleverer than I thought. She wants a life of royalty so she can sit around, 'trying' to look pretty and sweet and have others wait on her. She cares nothing for the prince."

"A bit like you, wouldn't you say?"

His eyes bored into hers, making her think his semi-pleasant demeanor might change suddenly if she wasn't careful.

"I care about Prince Valian," she said in a small whisper, looking up at him, trying to bat her eyes, but her feelers were making it difficult. They would let go of her eyes and dart about her face, looking for moisture. She kept trying to wipe them off, swatting at them like a pesky fly.

Maximillion began to chuckle.

Violet, frustrated, gave him a stubborn look.

"It's not funny . . ." she began.

"Yes, it is," Maximillion retorted. "I think it's ready for you to drink," he said, losing interest.

Violet hurried to the pot and lifted it to her lips. Her feelers seemed to sense something and began thrashing violently as if trying to get away, to remove themselves from her forehead.

She paused and then began to sip the liquid. It tasted salty, almost overwhelmingly salty.

Her feelers suddenly became stiff as nails, standing straight up in the air.

As she continued to drink, they slowly began to get shorter and shorter, like they were melting away.

Violet finished the last swallow and lifted her shaking hands to her face. She felt all over. The tentacles were gone, and so were the welts.

Violet ran to the mirror and breathed a sigh of relief. She giggled with delight as the dark patches on her face and arms began to fade and soon disappeared. She looked like her old self again.

Hesitantly, she walked back into the room.

Maximillion was standing at the window.

"What was it I drank? And what caused me to grow those . . . things?"

"You grew tentacles because snails eat dirt and black Peruvian toadstools. That is why you craved the soil you were about to eat. Likely, there were traces of snail droppings on the ones you picked. That is why you should have followed my instructions and used the blood of the toadstool. As far as what you drank . . . it was rock salt that you boiled. Salt will dry up and kill anything as fragile as a snail, or anything else for that matter, if taken in large enough doses. Now," he said, turning around, "do you have any sort of a plan?"

"Nothing specific," she answered, her voice quivering slightly, "but I am working on it. I'll try to get her alone, take a sail . . . and maybe we could "accidentally" run into you somewhere. You and her alone for a while . . . I'm sure you could work your magic quickly, and I would be free to show the prince what a waste of time she is."

A devilish grin grew over Maximillion's face.

"I like it," he said, staring at her. "You just let me know the time and place and I will be waiting."

"You know, I just thought of something," she said. "Haley seemed to be quite taken by Tilly at the meeting the other night; that is, she seemed to really be interested in her. Perhaps you could use Tilly's influence?"

"Yes . . . yes . . . outstanding. Possibly an invitation from Tilly might be the answer."

"Yes," said Violet with a devious smile.

"Yes, I think I'll suggest it to her casually . . . " he trailed off.

"It's settled then," said Violet confidently. "I'll see what I can do on my end for your . . . success," she added.

"How did you become so devious?" Maximillion asked. "None of the other fairies I've met even come close to your nastiness."

"I'm not a Manwan," she replied with a grin. "I don't have a given gem to control my emotions and actions."

Maximillion tilted his head in thought.

"You may be more useful than I anticipated," he said.

Violet cringed.

"What do you mean?" she asked.

"I don't know yet, but I'm sure I'll think of something," he answered, throwing his cloak over his shoulders. "Well, I'm off . . . now that I've done my good deed for this century. I'll be in touch," he said with an intense stare.

He turned and shot out the door, riding a pitch-black broom. She didn't even see where it came from; he was so quick.

She walked back to the mirror, admiring her looks when it dawned on her. "How in blazes did he shrink small enough to fit into my cottage?" she asked herself. She shrugged her shoulders and began practicing her smile in the mirror.

"I'll get the prince if it's the last thing I do! Mirror, mirror on the wall," she laughed wickedly at her reflection.

Violet spent most of the next morning primping in front of the mirror, choosing her best gown, trying different hairstyles, and preparing a little speech. An apology of sorts for Valian and Haley, to try and get back in their good graces, fall on their mercies. She was sure it would work, especially since Haley had taken pity on her at Mathilda's.

She fanned her wings enticingly in front of the mirror.

"What does she have that I haven't got?" she asked herself, batting her eyes. "Nothing, absolutely nothing."

With a satisfied nod, she went to the door. It was noon when she arrived at Mathilda's for a bite to eat. She hoped there was no one there that would remember what happened yesterday.

It was a beautiful day, and she took a table on the food court outside.

As the brownie walked away with her order, she looked out over the valley with a satisfied sigh.

High above the valley floor, eight little dots appeared on the horizon, flying high. As they drew closer, they flew over Mathilda's, heading south.

Violet recognized Valian's great wing span and saw, with disappointment, Haley right beside him, along with six others. She noticed they were all girded with knapsacks as they passed overhead.

The brownie came shuffling over with her food.

"Can I have that to go?" she asked as she watched the party land at the top of the canyon.

The brownie mumbled something inaudible and shuffled back inside.

"Now, where are they headed?" she said under her breath. "Looks like they're taking a little trip."

She gazed up at the cliffs with a scowl.

The brownie came out with a small sack and plopped it on the table.

"I'm kind of in a hurry; can you put this on my tab, please?"

He rolled his eyes and whipped out a notebook, made an entry, turned with a grunt, and went back inside.

Violet watched the top of the canyon for any sign of movement.

After several minutes, two witches rose into the air and sped off on their brooms, heading right for her as the group at the canyon's top rose and disappeared over the trees.

Estelle and Hilda landed at the food court just behind her.

She had her back to them and pretended to be busy with her food sack as they took seats at the next table.

"I pray they are successful . . . " Estelle was saying as she propped up her broom.

"They will be," Hilda replied. "They are the best guardians in the land."

Violet leaned just slightly so she wouldn't miss a word.

"I do hope the queen is alright," said Estelle.

"I know," Hilda agreed. "There would be uproar in Roan if anyone knew."

Violet's eyes moved back and forth at the implication of their words. She would follow the group and thwart their efforts or maybe she would be the one to rescue the queen from whatever peril she was in, and the rewards . . . she grinned to herself and quietly rose into the air and flew down the canyon. Glancing back, she saw that neither witch paid any attention.

As soon as she was sure they were out of range, she changed directions and shot up the canyon wall, hovering just below the crest, listening.

When she couldn't hear any voices she popped up and landed on the dirt path. After a quick look around, she took flight up over the trees.

Up ahead in the distance she could see a tall glittering tower with two individuals standing there.

She hovered and watched them. One at a time, they stepped into the tower and disappeared.

Quickly she shot toward the swirling mass. When she arrived, she waited for several minutes. Had she been paying attention, she would have noticed the two had changed size; however, seeing them at such a distance, it never occurred to her they were small.

"It's now or never," she said to herself as she stepped into the brightly shining vortex.

Violet had never been to the human side before and had no idea what to expect. She tried not to pay too much attention to her surroundings and kept her eye on the small dot which was growing larger and larger until she was thrust out the other end.

Immediately, she was in pain. She was smack dab in the middle of some thorny bush. It took her a good half an hour to get out without causing too much damage; still, her wings had small tears in them.

She stood in the dark, examining her left wing. She was twisted toward the left with her wing in her hands, rubbing on the tears gently as if rubbing a sore spot. Her arms were all scratched up and she was bleeding from a small cut on her cheek.

Violet examined her other wing and then looked around. She couldn't see anything except a tiny light shining in the distance.

Chapter Nine

DUELING PRINCES

Haley, Valian, and their guardians flew most of the day, taking their time and not saying much. They didn't cover as much ground as they would have had they not changed size.

They were worried about the queen but knew they couldn't be seen so they kept close to the canopies of the vast forests, taking advantage of the natural cover.

Haley marveled at the breathtaking views of majestic, snow covered mountain tops and crystal clear lakes.

The land was unspoiled and wild. Green meadows and flower-filled fields were abundant. She could see herself and Valian exploring the land together sometime in the future, whenever they finally solved this mystery.

At dusk, Valian found an old hollowed out tree and suggested they stop to rest.

Haley got comfortable on a pile of straw and down, the remnants of an old bird nest.

Valian finally introduced their guardians.

Celio had jet-black, curly hair and gray eyes. He was tall, slender, and muscular, just like all the guardians, and had wings so light in color they were almost invisible except for the blue edges.

Lonato had red hair, light green eyes, and a face full of freckles.

The guys made a small fire and cooked up a pot of stew.

Haley was always surprised at the efficiency of the Manwans. They always seemed to be totally prepared, and she found it curious the diversity of equipment that could fit in the smallest of knapsacks. She smiled and shook her head.

"What?" Valian asked.

"You amaze me," she answered, motioning to the stew pot.

"What's so amazing?" his eyes gleaming with wonder. "After all, we're not just ordinary beings; we're fairies endowed with the knowledge of the mystical arts of magic."

"Yes, I understand that," she said, a little forlorn, "it's just . . . that's something I will never be able to do."

"You won't need to," he said, with that handsome smile that made her go weak in the knees. "I will provide for your every need."

She gazed into his eyes.

"You're such a gentleman," she sighed.

They ate their stew and settled down for about a three-hour nap. Valian wanted to get up and go while it was still dark.

Several hours later, he was gently shaking her.

"What a pleasant awakening," she smiled sleepily.

"It's time to hit the skies," he said.

She could see the excitement on his face.

"You're awfully chipper for this early," she commented.

She didn't think she'd ever seen him look more human than at that moment. His emotions just added something more to his already wonderful disposition.

He pulled out the map Henry had found and examined it again.

"Pretty soon, we'll be leaving familiar lands into the unknown," he said, his brow creased in concentration. "The fairy farm is just an hour away, after that I don't know," he added with a grin.

"Fairy farm, what's that?"

"It's a wonderful place. They house all the animals there, and there are many, many crops of all types."

"You mean like a dairy farm like we have back home?" she asked with a frown. "I thought you said you didn't kill animals for food."

"We don't," Valian chuckled. "It's a place where they are studied and . . . I don't know the word . . . duplicated. No, that's not it. I can't explain it, but we get eggs and milk, vegetables, and a lot of other stuff from there. There are miles and miles of rolling hills covered in crops. Corn, wheat, beans, tomatoes, peas, potatoes; you name it, every kind of natural food you can think of oh, and let's not forget fruit. We have trees of every kind, vines, and a whole host of fairies that take care of it from seedling to harvest. There's squash, pumpkins, and melons . . . they provide for the entire land of Roan and beyond."

"Wow," Haley said, softly. "I can't wait to see it."

"We should be there around sun up."

The group gathered up their supplies.

Celio and Lonato yawned, trying to wake up. As they departed the tree, the cold pre-dawn air perked them right up.

Since it was still dark, they changed to their larger size so they could cover more ground.

The skies were cloud covered; not a star was in sight. It was just slightly humid, making it feel cold to Haley, and she shivered almost uncontrollably as they flew.

Valian could see she was struggling, so they stopped.

"Here, this will help," he said, reaching into her knapsack and pulling out a very unique sweater. It was shaped like a halter top and fastened at the back. It had long sleeves and almost no weight.

He helped her into it, and at once, she was completely toasty.

"Amazing," she said, delighted.

They took off, flying high in the sky to avoid hitting anything they couldn't see, and made good time, covering a great distance.

The sunrise was spectacular. The sky was bright orange and pink as it crested the horizon. Night dew glimmered all around them.

The fields turned golden as the first rays kissed them good morning and the clouds began to break up. Light purple and blue patches appeared in the sky like a quilt.

Haley breathed deeply.

The air was crisp and exhilarating. Joy filled her heart at the scene before her and the man beside her.

She took his hand, and they rejoiced in each other as the land passed by beneath them. Her stomach started to growl so loud she was sure the others could hear it.

"There it is, up ahead!" Valian said excitedly, "Fairy Farm. I haven't been here for ages. We can't stay long, but you have to see it."

His smile gave Haley a contentment she'd never felt before.

The days were growing shorter, and autumn was taking its first peek at the land. The trees were just at the beginning stages of turning color.

"I'd forgotten how beautiful . . . " Valian trailed off. "Too soon, the harvest will be over, and snow will come," he said with a sigh. "I love the seasons, don't you?"

"I didn't know it snowed here," Haley said, surprised. "I love the snow."

"So do I," he said, giving her hand a squeeze.

"I like to walk through a quiet forest when it's snowing those big, fat, lazy flakes, you know when they fall really slowly."

Valian smiled.

"You like the outdoors and adventure, just like me. When this is all over, we'll have to really take a sail; a long one, just you and I, and we'll explore realms I've never seen."

"Yes, I'd love that," Haley smiled.

She heard the sound of honking and looked up to see a flock of geese heading southward.

They flew in low, landing on a wide, dusty street. It reminded Haley of the old west, the way the buildings were lined up, connected to each other with covered wooden boardwalks like sidewalks.

There were dozens of buildings, large and small, along the road. The place was buzzing with activity as fairies and brownies and some creatures Haley had never seen before milled about, going about their business.

She was all smiles and breathed in the scent of freshly mowed hay and manure.

"It's just like back home," she said, beaming. "I love farms."

Valian grabbed her hand and took her on a tour.

They visited the cow barn, where dozens of cows were being milked and the sheep shed, where the sheep had already developed fine, new winter wool coats. They saw goats, chickens, and a large green pasture filled with fine steeds, galloping together in groups as if playing while the colts romped around with glee, leaping about.

Haley climbed up the wooden fence and watched them, delighted. She could have stayed there all day, but Valian took her by the arm.

"Come . . . there's more to see," he said with a satisfied look.

They headed for the other end of the plantation, where a whole host of fairies were harvesting. Multitudes of different foods were being picked, dug up, and chopped off simultaneously.

Haley was amazed at how organized everyone was and the ease of what they were doing.

There were no tractors or combines, just simple tools like shovels and hoes, which had obviously been charmed.

Some of the workers were only pointing and directing with their fingers, and some, Haley saw with astonishment, were using what she was sure were wands.

She looked up at Valian and then back at the harvesters.

"Those aren't . . . "

Valian looked over to where she was gazing with wonder.

"What?" he asked.

"Those aren't . . . are those wands?"

Valian chuckled softly.

"Yes, those are wands."

She gave him a questioning look and he explained.

"Some species don't have the same capabilities as Manwans. Those are Fairies of the Wood. Their population spans thousands of miles."

Haley shook her head.

"Have you ever heard of Tinker Bell?" he asked.

She turned toward him in shock. Her mouth dropped open.

"Tink . . . Tinker Bell?"

He nodded, and Haley began to laugh.

"Are you kidding me? Tinker Bell? I learned that fairy tale when I was four years old!"

"A fairy tale for you," Valian replied, "but reality for us. Tinker Bell is the queen of the Fairies of the Wood."

"Oh, my gosh, I'd love to meet her!" Haley said, thoroughly excited, clapping her hands and jumping up and down at the prospect of meeting a real fairy tale fairy.

"I'll try to arrange it," said Valian. "She is a very busy queen; it won't be easy."

"Oh, if you could . . . that would make my day."

"I'll see what I can do."

They continued to watch the workers harvest for a while until Haley's stomach began to growl again.

Valian looked at her.

"Are you ready for breakfast?"

"Yes, I am starved."

"Come on," he said, taking her by the hand.

They walked back down to the boardwalk.

Haley admired the little shops along the way.

They stopped at a diner and went in for breakfast.

It was very small, with wood planked floors that squeaked and groaned as they walked. There were a dozen stools in front of a long counter.

They took their seats as a robust fairy came out of the kitchen.

"Good morning," he said, wiping his hands on his apron.

Haley wrinkled her nose at how dirty his apron was and hoped it wasn't an indication of how the food would be.

When he saw Valian, he broke out in a wide, toothy grin.

"Your Highness," he said, reaching across the counter to shake Valian's hand. "It has been too long."

Valian smiled.

"Indeed, it has. Buggsy, I would like you to meet Haley Miles."

Buggsy took Haley's hand.

"How do you do?" she smiled.

He stared at her with pleasure.

"You are strikingly attractive," he said without missing a beat.

Haley blushed.

"Don't get any ideas, Buggs; she's my betrothed," said Valian with a small chuckle.

Buggsy didn't seem to have heard a word as he held Haley's hand.

"Buggsy!" said Valian, loudly, snapping him out of his little trance.

"Huh?" he said, looking back at Haley, flashing her a grin.

Celio and Lonato rolled their eyes, smirking.

"Haley and I are to be married," said Valian.

"Oh . . . oh!" he said, letting go of her hand.

"Well, congratulations!" he grinned at Valian. "You've got excellent taste. Well, what can I get you, folks? We've got a special today: oatmeal with raisins and brown sugar, with plenty of fresh butter, toast, and rainbow dew."

Haley smiled at his enthusiasm.

"That sounds . . . filling," she replied, "I'll have that, thank you."

"I'll have the same," said Valian.

It was oatmeal all around.

Buggsy went back into the kitchen while a very small fairy brought them their drinks. She was so small that she had to fly to reach the countertop and use her wand to direct their mugs.

"My name is Tweet," she said, smiling shyly.

"How do you do Tweet," Haley responded. "Are you of the fairies of the wood?"

Tweet nodded. She was very attractive; long golden locks and vivid, hazel eyes, and the longest eyelashes Haley had ever seen.

Haley smiled as she sipped her rainbow dew. It was the freshest she'd tasted yet.

"Umm, this is wonderful."

"It's made with the freshest of oranges from these groves," said Valian. "Unfortunately, it loses its punch so quickly during transport."

Buggsy came out with four bowls of oatmeal, and the group ate quickly like they hadn't had a meal in weeks.

Haley appreciated Valian's healthy appetite and wondered how the removal of his given gem could affect him in such a way.

When they were finished, Valian and the guardians arranged to pay for their meals by helping with spring planting.

Haley looked at her husband-to-be curiously.

"I can help, too," she said.

Valian looked at her tenderly.

"You are my betrothed. I wouldn't think of asking you to help."

"I insist," she replied. "I'm not a freeloader, and I'm certainly not afraid of work."

He smiled.

"If you wish it, then it will be so."

The group said their goodbyes and left the diner with full bellies and satisfied smiles, ready for the journey ahead.

They traveled for a couple of days, only stopping to rest and eat.

The countryside was splendid. Valian and Haley were enjoying the trip and each other immensely. The further they went, the warmer it became, and Haley had to put away her sweater.

The scenery began to change as well. They flew over miles and miles of forest, unbroken by lakes or wide open spaces, until they began to thin and were replaced by more tropical vegetation.

Abundant, lush, and green plant life featured large, dazzling, exotic blooms in every color. The landscape revealed a growing presence of palm trees.

Crystal clear pools and majestic waterfalls were abundant, and among the brilliant colored flowers were towering ferns in every shape, size, and color of green.

They came upon a pool so beautiful that Haley insisted they stop for a break and take a dip in the deep, blue water.

Valian was hesitant at first, but when he saw the disappointment on her face, he had to give in.

"I must admit," he confessed with a hint of uncertainty, "the experience is entirely unfamiliar to me; I've never been swimming before."

"Neither have we," the guardians replied.

Haley shook her head.

"Unbelievable," she said, taking Valian by the hand.

"Look, it's not deep here," she said, leading him in.

The water was warm, and it felt good on her feet.

Valian began to relax and walked up the shoreline as Haley waded in further.

"Wait!" Valian yelled, suddenly alarmed. "Your wings… you can't get them wet!"

"What do you mean?" she yelled back. "We fly in the rain, what's the difference?"

"Oh yeah," Valian replied with a look of embarrassment. "Sorry, I wasn't thinking."

"Yes, you were," said Haley, with a thumb up as she dove in.

"Haley?"

When she didn't come up right away, he yelled again, beginning to panic.

"Haley!"

She popped her head up on the other side of the pool.

"Wow! That was great!"

He shook his head.

"I don't like that!" he called.

The fear on his face brought Haley back down to earth quickly, and she rose out of the pool and flew to him.

"I'm sorry," she said, giving him a hug. "I sometimes forget you're new to these sorts of things."

She looked into his pale blue eyes, water dripping from her nose, her dark hair hanging in wet strings.

Valian lifted her up and twirled her around.

"I adore you," he said, laughter in his eyes. "I can see being married to you will never be boring."

Haley laughed as he twirled her in circles.

"Stop, you're making me dizzy!" she laughed.

He set her down, and they went and sat in the sun to dry.

She fanned her wings and combed out the tangles in her hair.

Valian watched her contentedly as she tended to herself.

"I am totally in love," he said happily, putting his arm around her. "I can't wait for the day you become my wife. I will be complete."

She smiled up at him.

"The feeling's mutual," she said and kissed him on the cheek.

He turned, looking for Celio and Lonato.

"Come on you two, it's time to get going."

The guardians came out from behind a hedge of trees. Each was holding a single lily and promptly presented them to Haley.

She smiled and thanked them as she fastened one into her hair.

Valian threw the guardians a grateful look. They, in turn, gave each other a high five, which made Haley laugh.

"You've got the hang of it!"

"We've been practicing," said Lonato.

"Is everybody ready?" Valian asked.

Everyone gave a thumbs up, and they took flight.

At sunset, they caught their first glimpse of the ocean.

Haley could smell the salt in the air and thought it gave off the best fragrance. She watched in awe as the waves crashed against the rocks and as the sea birds floated on the wind currents. She wanted very much to walk on the beach, but Valian thought it too dangerous while it was still light out.

The group watched the sunset. The horizon was ablaze in deep reds and oranges, and the stars began to appear one by one

The waves rushed in and out, stopping just before they reached the group. They sat, mesmerized by the sounds and smells.

"I've never seen the ocean before," said Valian, in a soft whisper, as if talking aloud would somehow spoil the magic of this place.

"Me neither," Haley whispered back. "It's a first for the both of us. A memory we can share."

They both felt at peace.

Celio and Lonato sat silent, they're eyes glued to the magnificence before them. Soon darkness fell, and the only light to guide them was the moon and the stars.

They silently took flight, scanning the water carefully for any dark land mass ahead.

Haley saw something looming into view and gave Valian's arm a tug and pointed.

It slowly grew larger as they neared. They could make out forests of palm trees and dark sandy beaches.

Slowly, they flew over the island, looking for any sign of life. It was full of sound.

Haley could hear the cries of night birds and the sounds of what she thought could be monkeys. The place was teaming with activity, but it was all animal sound.

As they circled the island, Valian spotted light far ahead in the distance. It looked like a flickering fire. He hovered as the others turned to look.

"That must be them," Haley said, quietly.

"Let's go," he said.

With a strong beat of his wings, he shot ahead of the others. Haley desperately tried to keep up, but her wings weren't as powerful as the others, and she fell behind. By the time she caught up, they had already landed on a large palm on the beach.

"Slow down next time," she whispered.

"Sorry, I'm just anxious to find Mother and punish these fugitives," Valian whispered back.

She patted him on the shoulder and looked up at the beach. She could see figures sitting around a campfire. There were half a dozen grass huts on the shore just above the sand dunes, nestled along the tree line.

Two figures emerged from one of the huts, and Haley's heart began to pound. One had a tall, pointed hat on, and a long black cloak trailed behind the other. She held her breath.

"Closer," she whispered, leaping from the palm before Valian could stop her.

There was no mistaking it. It was Maximillion and Tilly laughing it up. The others on the beach sat in their chairs, amused at the horseplay.

Before she realized what was happening, Valian shot out from behind her, his sword in hand and his jaw locked.

He landed in front of the group, spraying sand at their feet. Maximillion swung around in surprise and looked Valian dead in the face. He was as calm as the surface of a still pond.

"Prince Valian . . . what do we owe the pleasure of this visit?" he asked in a playful, dangerous voice.

The others stood quickly upon Valian's arrival.

Maximillion looked past Valian; his eyes focused on Haley perched at the top of the palm.

Valian was silent as if struggling for the right words.

"Milady, please join us with your lovely presence," said Maximillion with delight.

Haley hovered, sat back down, and then hovered again, fighting against the urge to heed Maximillion's beckoning. His invitation seemed to motivate Valian into a response.

"What's going on here . . ." he stammered, "why are you on this island?"

Maximillion gave him a 'it's none of your business look.'

"Not that it's any of your concern; we come to this island every year for a siesta before the harvest and All Hallows Eve, and you may sheath your sword . . . you won't be needing it."

Valian looked uncertain.

One of the witches removed her hood, and he took a step back in surprise. It was Hilda. She had a grim look on her face.

She approached the two as they stared at each other, each determined to be the victor in whatever transpired.

"Now you two take it easy," she said, inching her way forward; ready to jump between them.

Valian glared at the sorcerer.

"Haley is my betrothed. Don't even think of using your magic on her," he growled.

"You're not married; she's fair game," Maximillion replied with a sneer.

Valian took a step forward. The two were almost nose to nose.

Haley was still up in the tree. She felt confused. It was like her emotions were being yanked back and forth from Valian to Maximillion and back again. She had strong feelings for Valian and felt proud and special as she watched him defend her honor, yet she felt pulled somehow, like a puppet on a string, toward the dark and mysterious sorcerer.

Hilda was trying desperately to get between the two, but neither would budge.

They stood firm, looking each other in the eye.

"Fair game?" said Valian, "you speak of her as if she were just some little conquest of yours, some kind of prize."

"Oh, but she is," Maximillion replied, "she is a prize worth fighting for."

Valian's ears turned red, and his chest rose as his breathing quickened; his muscles flexed and twitched, ready to strike.

"If you insist," he said, raising his sword, as the sorcerer threw his cloak over his shoulder.

"Stop!" Hilda yelled. "You will stop this at once!"

Maximillion grew red in the face and took a step back.

Haley sat in the palm, her heart pounding. She rose from her perch and flitted down to stand by Hilda. They exchanged glances.

Valian didn't back down.

"You're pathetic. I wouldn't want to waste my time."

Maximillion's face grew into a grimace at the insult.

Hilda and Haley wrinkled their noses. "Ooh," they said under their breath, taking a step back.

"Pathetic . . . you're the pathetic one, flitting about in your little dress, parading around with your chest heaved forward like you're the big man in the realm, fanning your little wings, oh look at me, I'm the prince," Maximillion said, mockingly.

Valian's eyes became narrow.

"I could snap your neck in an instant, you overgrown little sissy," he said, glaring at the sorcerer.

The others stood, fascinated at the verbal bashing taking place before them. Several were trying to hide smiles and smirks on their faces. They had never seen the likes of it before, two princes' trying to outwit each other with words. Neither had ever been in an exchange such as this, and Haley didn't think they knew what to do.

"I ought to . . ." Valian began and lunged at Maximillion so suddenly it took him by surprise. He gave the sorcerer a forceful shove.

Maximillion fell backward, tripping over his cloak, and landed on his backside.

Valian stood there triumphantly; his wings spread wide.

Maximillion got up, brushed himself off, and swung at Valian, hitting him smack in the jaw, then yelped at the pain in his hand.

"Whoa!" cried several in the group.

"Get him!" someone yelled.

All bets were off. The two lunged at each other and were soon rolling on the ground, throwing blows, punching, and kicking.

Maximillion had hold of Valian's golden locks and was pulling with all his might while Valian was half strangling the sorcerer with his own cloak.

Haley watched with growing concern. She didn't like fights. She never had.

"Stop it!" she yelled.

They paid her no mind.

"Please! Cut it out!"

Her words were unheard as the princes continued to pummel each other. She suddenly had an idea.

Haley quickly dashed up to the mass of arms and legs and yanked the bow and arrows from Valian's waist. She pulled a very small arrow from the quiver and took aim. Hilda put out her hand to stop her.

"What are you doing?" she cried.

"It's alright," said Haley, showing her the arrow.

Hilda raised an eyebrow.

"That isn't . . . is that . . . ?"

Haley grinned.

Maximillion looked up at her from under Valian's leg and put out his hand as if to shield himself as she drew back the string and fired, grazing Valian's arm and hitting Maximillion square in the chest. The twisting and thrashing stopped quickly.

The two lay there motionless.

She looked at the pair of them; fear, disappointment, and uncertainty written across her face. When they didn't move, she was afraid she'd killed them.

Maximillion moaned as he tried to push Valian off. The arrow was so small it hadn't caused any physical damage.

"Huh?" he said, scratching his head.

He looked down and pulled the arrow from his chest, making a sound like a high-pitched guitar string.

Haley had an amused look on her face and had to look away before she began to laugh.

Both princes scratched their heads, confused and bewildered. When their eyes met, Maximillion broke out in a grin.

The rest of the group didn't understand what just happened, but Hilda and Haley were all smiles.

The princes slowly got up, brushing themselves off, and Maximillion began to laugh.

Hilda gave Haley a high five.

"Attagirl," she said. "That'll teach em'."

Haley smiled.

"Do you mind if I sit?" she asked.

"Not at all," Hilda replied, sitting down herself. Cupid's arrow, huh? Nice touch."

Haley grinned.

"For a moment there, I thought I killed them."

Hilda laughed.

"For a moment there, I thought you'd lost your mind."

Valian took a seat in one of the chairs, trying to catch his breath, watching Maximillion as he stood there grinning.

As the realization took hold of what had just happened, he looked over at his bride-to-be, impressed at her quick thinking and level-headedness.

"How long before the effects wear off, do you think?" Haley asked, looking at Hilda.

"I have no idea. I've never seen it done before," she replied.

"Well, let's get down to business before it does," said Haley. "So, you are all on a siesta?"

"Yes. Every year, we come here to relax and reflect. Imagine my surprise when you showed up. What are you doing here?"

Haley explained about Henry finding the map, which led them to believe the queen may have been taken to one of the islands.

"She isn't here," said Hilda.

Haley looked over at the princes and marveled at the effects of Cupid's arrow.

Maximillion was obviously not in love, but he acted like he and Valian were the best of friends.

"Well," she sighed, "it looks like this is a dead end."

"You'd best get Valian out of here before he comes to his senses," she said, motioning toward Maximillion.

"Well . . . thank you," said Haley.

Hilda smiled that kind of motherly smile.

"Good luck," she said, giving Haley a hug. "I know you will find her."

"Thanks, we will. Come on, guys. Let's regroup and decide what to do."

As they took flight, Haley glanced back and giggled to herself as Maximillion waved goodbye. She suddenly wondered what in the world she saw in him.

The trip back to Roan was uneventful.

Valian questioned her about what had happened with Maximillion. He was rather embarrassed by his actions and didn't understand why.

"I'm sorry about that. I hope you don't feel bad. It's just that you were fighting for no reason," she explained.

"I don't understand," Valian said, frowning.

"You were fighting out of jealousy. There was no need. I care for you, and I wouldn't leave you for anyone."

She began to giggle again.

"You were fighting like a couple of girls."

"It was my first time," Valian reasoned. "I have fought many battles but this was quite different."

"That's okay," Haley said with a loving look. "You displayed an emotion that is quite common on our side. It can be very destructive. Jealousy will eat away at a person and poison them. No good can come from it."

"I can't help how I feel."

"I understand that, and you will have these types of feelings, but you have to learn not to react in such a manner. As I said, I wouldn't leave you for such a man. Your reaction showed a lack of trust in me and how I feel about you."

"I didn't realize . . . I am sorry," Valian said sadly.

"It's alright," Haley said gently, taking him by the hand.

"This is a new kind of battle. The only way you will learn is by experience, just like Henry and I have."

"Yes, I'm afraid so," he agreed.

They continued their journey home without incident and arrived back at the palace mid-afternoon.

A visibly shaken guardian met them.

"What's going on?" Valian asked.

"Sir Valian . . . I am so glad you're back, the whole city has gone crazy," the guardian stuttered.

"What do you mean?" Haley asked with growing concern.

"The fairies have been breaking out in fights. There has been crying from most of the females and the children . . . the children are out of control and have been fighting amongst themselves, being disobedient and hysterical. We don't know what to do. We tried to call an assembly, but only half showed up, and even then, no one could agree on anything. Half the citizens have been dueling and actually physically hitting each other."

Valian and Haley exchanged knowing looks. The guardians had never been warned about the consequences of removing their given gems. Valian looked back at the guardian.

"Call an assembly by my order for tomorrow morning."

"How long has it been like this?" Haley asked.

"It started a couple of days after you left. Just a couple fights at first, then it escalated into brawls, then all-out riots."

Haley shook her head.

"Maybe we should have everyone put their gems back on," she suggested.

"We can't," Valian answered.

"Why not?"

"Because the queen ordered it. Only she can give the order."

"Can't you override it? You're the prince."

"I don't know. I guess so."

"I think we should do it, just for a little while, and give the fairies an opportunity to be told what's happening to them and how to deal with it. Then let them have the choice of whether or not they will wear their gems."

Valian cocked his head, contemplating her suggestion.

"I don't think your mother fully realized what would happen after she gave the order, and if she were here, she would probably agree to have everyone put their gems back on. What do you think?"

Valian nodded.

He instructed the guardian to tell the entire kingdom to put their gems back on immediately.

The guardian took flight as ordered.

"Let's go get something to eat and then go pay a visit to Zeb and Sarah," said Valian. "I think we will need all the help we can get in this matter. Perhaps they will join us in teaching everyone about the dangers and the joys that are experienced by the removal of the gems. After that, we have to continue the hunt for Mother. It is critical we find her and soon, but we can't leave Roan in this condition. We wouldn't have a kingdom to come back to."

The couple went directly to the kitchen. When they arrived, they found all the brownies gathered together, having an intense discussion.

As the prince entered the room, they all stood. The room was silent.

"Your . . . Your Highness . . ." one of the brownies stuttered in surprise. "We were just talking about all the trouble we've seen."

"Be of good cheer," said Valian. "We know what's been happening, and it is being rectified as we speak. We will be holding an assembly tomorrow morning after breakfast, so I would like to see the best food possible. They will all need to recover their strength after this ordeal. In the meantime, Haley and I are starved."

The brownies quickly put together a meal, and they ate right there in the kitchen.

Haley looked around at the brownies' workplace. It was an enormous room. It looked just like a kitchen you would see in a restaurant.

Stoves and griddles were lined up in rows, and coolers filled with freshly made salads, desserts, and fruit were positioned against the back wall.

Then there were the solid butcher block tables used for rolling out pie crusts and all manner of baking. Tall ovens were lined up against the far wall, and pots, pans, and utensils hung from large racks over a center preparation table. Over in a corner were two very large dishwashers with plastic racks full of clean, sparkling dishes, ready to be put away.

The entire room had the cleanest shine Haley had ever seen, and she was impressed at the efficiency of the staff.

They finished eating and stood to leave. Just then, the head brownie walked over.

"Where is the queen?" he asked, almost suspiciously.

Without batting an eye, Valian replied.

"She is still on retreat and will be joining us when she is ready."

The firmness in his voice seemed to quell any further inquiry, and the brownie turned back to his duties, mumbling quietly under his breath.

Valian and Haley exchanged glances and quickly left the room.

They went to the blue room and rehearsed what they would say the next morning. They tried to anticipate what kind of questions would be asked, then decided to visit Zeb and Sarah later.

By the time Haley got to her room, she was exhausted. She took a hot bath and climbed into bed, rehearsing her speech to the fairies as she drifted off.

Chapter Ten

AN AWAKENING

Henry, Sersha, and the two guardians quietly watched Ike and the stranger.

Sersha suddenly turned, putting her hand on Henry's arm.

"Shh," she whispered, "we're not alone."

Henry looked around.

"I don't see anyone," he replied quietly, looking back at the shed.

Ike had locked up his shed and was turning to leave. The map was clearly visible, sticking out of his back pocket.

"Come on," Henry whispered.

The four quietly flew to the roof of the house, where they could watch from a distance.

Ike and the stranger disappeared inside the house.

"What are we going to do now?" Sersha asked.

"Let's go check out my parents," Henry replied.

"Alright, there's not much we can do here."

They took off, Henry leading the way.

His heart began to pound with excitement as they flew over the Kootenai River, across the meadow to the top of the bluff where the Miles' estate sat perched on the edge of the cliff.

Henry could see the moon's reflection in the dark tower windows. The sight of his home warmed his heart. He and Haley had barely had the chance to get to know this place before Sersha's first appearance at Haley's bedroom window, which seemed like a lifetime ago.

He began to perspire, and he wondered about the weather. He couldn't understand how the seasons changed so quickly. It was the beginning of June when they arrived back in Roan; now it seemed like it was the middle of summer.

"I'll never understand how time works," he said as they approached the east tower.

Sersha smiled. "You probably never will. I don't know myself."

The four tiny figures zipped to the top of the east tower and peeked through the window. Henry smiled at his parents lying asleep in the moonlight.

"Are their memories still wiped out?" he whispered.

"Yes," Sersha answered.

He watched as his mother, Carol, turned over, slapped her pillow a couple of times, and laid her head back down. A cloud passed overhead, obscuring her face in shadow.

"Well," he said, "at least I know they are okay. Come on; we might as well go back to Ike's."

They arrived back at the bush across from Ike's shed. All was quiet.

"Let's see if we can find a way into that shed," said Henry. "We've got to get Valian's gem and the map if we can."

"Yes," Sersha agreed. "We've got to stop him from getting back into the fairy world."

The group began to look for a way in. As Henry rounded the back side of the shed, he spotted a vent near the top.

"Here," he whispered to the others. "I think we may be able to squeeze through here."

It was like sliding a hot knife through butter. All four slipped through the slats easily and found themselves hovering in the dark.

"We're gonna have to change size," said Henry.

The usual spark lit up the room.

"How are we going to get this open?" Henry was asking when he heard a clicking sound.

Everyone froze. Suddenly, the door slammed open. A dark silhouette stood in the moonlight and Henry knew at once it was Ike.

Immediately, everyone in the group shrank and headed for the vent.

Ike turned on the light and began to laugh.

"No, no, no, you can't get away."

The four were trying to jam their way through the slats, but something was blocking their exit.

They quickly changed back in size. Henry stood almost face to face with those cold eyes. His heart was pounding as he struggled for words.

"So . . ." said Ike, "you thought you would try and steal from me? Breaking and entering?" He paused, a malevolent smile forming.

"We're only taking back what you've stolen from us!" Sersha said defiantly, her hand on her sword.

Ike's eyes were drawn to her weapon.

"Go ahead, draw your sword," he taunted. "No one will ever miss you," he continued. "Who would believe? You're a figment of imagination."

"I'm not," Henry spoke up, hardness in his voice.

Henry was almost sixteen and was just as tall as Ike.

Ike sneered at the group.

"No one will miss you either," he snickered. "Your family has no memory of you, nor does anyone else," he snapped.

Doubt crossed Henry's face.

"How do you know . . . ?"

Just then, Ike stepped aside, revealing a beautiful blonde with striking violet eyes, wearing a triumphant smile on her face, along with the unknown stranger.

Sersha and Henry were stunned.

"You!" Sersha exclaimed. "What are you doing . . . you traitor! I should have known . . . "

Violet stepped inside. She walked up to Sersha and heaved out her chest proudly.

"So, the prince is betrothed . . . well, that's fine; I don't need him anymore," she said with contempt. "Ike here tells me I can and will have everything I've ever dreamed of on this side."

She turned, snapping her wing in Sersha's face.

Sersha didn't flinch as the cut next to her eye began to bleed, but her anger grew, and Henry sensed she might do something foolish. He gave her arm a nudge.

"How dare you deceive your kind . . . "

"My kind?" Violet mocked her angrily, "I am not your kind. You are an ignorant, pathetic breed. You think you are superior to everyone! You have all the answers and know what's best for all. And now you're experiencing emotion for the first time in your life? You wouldn't know real emotion if it bit you in the face!"

She snapped her wing again, cutting the other side of Sersha's face.

"I've wanted to do that a thousand times!" she laughed, turning to Ike.

Ike stood there, amused at Violet's taunting.

"I like your style," he said, looking at her affectionately.

"Thank you," she replied with a wicked smile.

"What shall we do with them?" she asked playfully.

"Search them, then lock them up," Ike answered, glaring at Henry.

"Turn around!" Violet commanded.

All four turned as Violet and the stranger began to frisk them.

"What's this?" the stranger asked excitedly as he pulled a smooth, blue stone from Henry's knapsack.

Violet quickly snatched it from his hand and inspected it closely.

"This is nothing," she said, tossing the blue stone to Ike.

Ike looked it over greedily, turning it in his hand.

"Maybe not," he said, raising an eyebrow.

He walked up to Henry and thrust it in his face.

"What is this?" he demanded.

Henry and Sersha exchanged looks.

"It's nothing," Henry answered, with just enough doubt in his voice to raise suspicion.

"What kind of gem is this?" Ike asked.

"It's not a gem," Henry answered. "It's . . . it's," he purposely struggled for words, "it's just a souvenir."

"Ah huh, a souvenir. Well, if I am to take you at your word and it's not a gem, perhaps it has magical properties?"

Ike watched Sersha and Henry exchange looks again.

Violet looked over at Ike and at the stone. She turned back to Sersha.

"Tell me," she said, whipping Sersha's sword from its sheath.

She held the sword to Sersha's throat.

"Tell me now, or you'll never draw another breath."

Sersha looked Violet straight in the eye.

"I'll never tell you anything, you filthy pig," she hissed and spit in Violet's face.

Startled, Violet staggered back a step. Fear was evident in her eyes as she wiped the spittle from her face. She had never seen this kind of defiance from a Manwan before. Angered, she raised the sword to strike.

"Wait!" Henry cried.

Violet paused and slowly turned to face him.

"Wait, I'll tell you, just don't hurt her," he pleaded.

"No, Henry, don't tell this sorry excuse for a fairy anything!" Sersha demanded angrily.

Henry ignored her.

"Let her go, and I'll tell you."

Violet turned to Ike.

"Let her go, and I'll tell you," she repeated in the snottiest voice she could muster.

In that moment as Violet took her eyes off them, Henry yelled.

"Change!"

Immediately, all four shrank, and with almost supernatural speed, they flew past their captors toward the open door.

Violet shrieked.

Ike shielded his face and ducked as Henry zipped past, but the stranger reached up and Sersha smashed into his hand, knocking herself into the wall as the other three flew out the door.

Henry hovered just out of reach, looking back at Sersha crumpled on the floor like a dead butterfly.

"Sersha!" he cried, preparing to fly back inside.

The guardians grabbed him and held him back.

"Go!" Sersha yelled, trying to get to her feet, just as Ike slammed an empty glass jar over her, trapping her inside.

"If you change, you will be cut to pieces by broken glass," he warned.

"Get them!" he snarled at the stranger.

"Leave them!" Violet interjected. "They can't find their way back to the other side without her," she said, looking at Sersha with a cold stare as Sersha trembled under the glass.

"My mother will have your wings for this when she finds out about your treachery."

"I happen to know the queen is missing," Violet interrupted. "She's probably dead," she continued with relish, "so keep your mouth shut!"

Violet turned to Ike.

"Let's go. We need to leave this place."

"I thought you said they couldn't find their way back to the other side…"

"They can't but there's no sense in taking any chances."

Ike nodded. He slid a piece of cardboard under the jar and picked up his prisoner.

"Come," he said. "I have a place we can go until we figure all this out."

Despite all Sersha's protests, Ike, Violet and the stranger left the shed and headed for the house.

"I have a hidden room in my basement. We'll go there and work on finding out what this stone is all about."

"Don't worry," said Violet. "I'll get it out of her.

Henry and the guardians retreated to the top of the hill and watched as Ike went back to the house.

"What are we going to do?" Theodore asked.

"We need to get help," Henry answered. "We've got to trick Ike into using the stone… somehow get Sersha to trick him. We can't leave her behind. I'm really afraid for her. Ike is dangerous."

Henry looked at the guardians. They looked extremely nervous and upset.

"Don't worry," said Henry, trying to comfort them. "We'll get her out of there. Do either of you know how to get back to the other side?" he asked.

"Yes," Troy answered, "but without my given a gem, I won't be able to see the portal when it appears."

"You'll just have to wing it," said Henry, chuckling at his wit. "Wait a minute; I've got a better idea. Let's go to my house and try using Estelle's postern. I'd almost forgotten about that. Here's what we'll do. Troy, you stay here and keep an eye out. Theodore and I will sneak into the estate. If this works, he will bring back help, and I will meet you back here as soon as I'm sure he's through. Theo, try to find Hilda and Estelle."

Theodore nodded.

Troy began to fidget.

"I'm feeling an odd sensation. I think I'm afraid," he said, wringing his hands.

"It's okay to be afraid. It will keep you on your toes and alert. Just stay hidden and you'll be fine. I won't be gone long, okay?"

Troy took a deep breath and nodded again.

"Let's go," said Henry, with a reassuring look at them both. "Don't worry, you're a guardian."

That seemed to do the trick as Troy thrust out his chest, a confident look crossing his face.

Henry and Theodore took off for the estate, flying as fast as they could. It would be light soon and Henry wanted to get in and out before sunrise.

They reached the estate, popped back to normal size and went to the back door. Henry turned the knob and breathed a sigh of relief when the door opened.

They snuck into the dark kitchen.

"Stay close," he whispered.

They arrived at Estelle's bedroom door and entered quickly. Henry spotted the large floor-to-ceiling picture. It was cold and gray looking.

"It looks like it's storming there," he said.

He grabbed one half dozen umbrellas stored in a wicker basket next to the postern.

"You'll need this. Find Estelle or Hilda and come back as soon as you possibly can."

"I will, Sir Henry," he said as he stepped into the postern.

He watched as Theodore disappeared into the picture. He could just vaguely make out the outline of his body as it blended into the gray.

He turned and walked back to the bedroom door when he heard a shuffling noise. He froze, wondering what would happen if he was discovered by one of his parents.

Their memories of him and Haley had been erased for the time being. Would they call the cops?

He decided that rather than get caught, he would go through the postern and return back with Theodore and Estelle.

He turned around, and as he did, the postern changed from a cold gray to almost pitch black.

Quite suddenly, Theodore and Estelle emerged, stepping into the room completely drenched.

He did a double take, rubbing his eyes to make sure he hadn't imagined it.

"Jumping jelly beans!" Estelle exclaimed, shaking the water from her cloak. "Towels," she commanded as two towels appeared out of thin air. She handed one to Theodore.

"We must hurry," she said as Henry stood there at a loss for words.

Just then, there was a knock at the door.

"Estelle?" Carol called as she opened the door.

It was so quick; no one had a chance to react.

Carol flipped on the light and looked from Estelle to Henry and at a dripping Theodore.

Theodore and Henry quickly shrouded their wings, but not quickly enough. Carol gasped and looked at Estelle.

"What's going on? Who are these people and . . . "

Estelle interrupted.

"It's alright, Mrs. Miles," she said as she walked toward her. "Come and sit down, and I'll tell you."

Carol looked almost frightened as she kept stealing glances at Henry and Theodore.

Estelle looked at Henry.

"We're gonna have to tell her," she said. We may need her help."

"Help?" Carol asked.

Henry nodded.

"Okay," he replied uncertainly.

"Henry . . . " Estelle began, as she motioned toward him; "is your son," she said, waving her hand in front of Carol's face.

Carol opened her mouth, but nothing came out as she studied Henry's face. A sudden realization came over her. She looked from Henry to Estelle, then at Theodore.

"I . . . I can't believe it," she stuttered. "I feel like I haven't seen you for years!"

"Okay, Mrs. Miles," Estelle began, "we have to fill you in, but we must be brief."

For the next fifteen minutes, Henry and Estelle gave a brief explanation about the land of Wisen, the fairies, and the heroic tale about Henry and Haley and Zeb's rescue and how the legend really happened.

By the time they were finished, Carol was reeling. The others stood there waiting for her to say something when she began to chuckle.

"You guys are good," she began. "You almost had me convin . . . "

Henry and Theodore unveiled their wings.

Carol let out a sound that resembled a small squeak.

Henry smiled at the look of shock on his mother's face.

"It's alright, Mom, it's me," he said as he walked towards her. "Come and look."

Carol gave him a bewildered look. She reached out a trembling finger and touched Henry's wing, drawing her hand back quickly as if it were hot.

"Oh, my goodness, it's true, it's all true. I'm at a loss for words. This is extraordinary! I can scarcely believe it!"

Henry continued to smile, as did Theodore and Estelle.

"It's so soft," she exclaimed, as she ran her hand up and down Henry's wing. "And this," she said, walking up to Estelle's postern. "This is a doorway to another world. I don't know what to say. I knew you two were up to something, always disappearing into the forest, but I never in my wildest dreams would have imagined this."

"There is so much more to tell you," said Estelle, "but we need to get going. We've got to get Sersha out of that man's house."

"Mr. Seers," said Carol. "I can't believe it. He seemed like such a nice man."

"Unfortunately, he isn't," said Henry.

"What can I do to help?" she asked.

"I've been thinking about that," Estelle replied. "I think if you paid him a visit, that would surely distract him enough. We may be able to get past him and get Sersha out of there before he realizes it."

"What about Violet?" Henry asked. "She's not that great, but she's still a fairy with magical powers."

"Yes, but don't forget, Sersha is also a fairy," said Estelle. "She is older, more experienced, and a Manwan, the oldest known species of fairy."

"There are many different species, all with their own magical talents, but the Manwan are the strongest. Violet will be no match for Sersha once she is free."

"Wait until Paul hears about this . . . what am I going to tell Paul?" Carol asked in a quandary. "He has to know. Maybe we'll pay Mr. Seers a visit together. Should I go wake him, and you break the news to him?"

"We haven't got time for that," said Henry. "You go ahead and wake him. Estelle, Theodore, and I will meet you there."

Carol looked apprehensive.

"How am I going to convince him about all this?" she asked.

"I've already restored his memory of the twins," said Estelle. "The rest will be up to you."

"Where's Haley?" Carol asked as they turned toward the door.

"She's with Valian on the other side, searching for the queen," Henry answered, opening the door.

"Come as soon as you can," said Estelle, grabbing her broom as she passed.

Carol followed them out the back kitchen door and watched Estelle mount her broom and take off like a shot.

Henry and Theodore spread their wings and dove over the side of the cliff, hot on Estelle's trail.

She stood there for several minutes as the three became small specks in the sky. She shook her head and had to pinch herself to be sure she wasn't dreaming, and then turned to go back inside to wake her unsuspecting husband.

Estelle, Theodore, and Henry arrived back at Ike's place and met up with Troy.

Henry instructed him to keep a lookout as Estelle began a wide sweep around the property.

Henry and Theodore changed size and zipped to the roof. All was dark and quiet except for a soft glow in a basement window.

He looked around for Estelle and spotted her hovering above the tree line. Her silhouette was classic witchlike: dark black, barely visible against the dark purple-blue, fast-approaching dawn.

Henry knew they must act quickly in locating Sersha and gave Estelle a heads up.

"Come on," he whispered.

He and Theodore dove over the edge of the roof and cautiously approached the basement window.

It was covered in a lacy, off-white curtain, and they could see through the gaps in the fabric.

Inside, across the room, a door stood ajar, spilling out a thin sliver of light. They could hear muffled voices.

Theodore suddenly tugged on Henry's arm and pointed out a gap between the foundation and the house. It was water damage from years of neglect and looked just large enough for them to squeeze through.

Henry had a look of uncertainty as he peered into the gap. He shook his head.

"Not a good idea," he whispered.

A thought suddenly crossed his mind, and he motioned to Theodore to follow.

They flew back up to the roof and over to the chimney.

"Let's try this way," he said quietly.

They descended the flue, hovering every foot or so, listening. When they reached the bottom, the damper was open just wide enough for them to drop through into the fireplace.

"Good thing it's summer," Henry whispered with a nervous smile.

The house was semi-dark inside as all the shades and curtains were closed. Several nightlights enabled them to make out their surroundings.

They were in a large living room. It seemed to be full of clutter. Dishes, cans, bottles, and potato chip bags covered almost every surface in the room.

The furnishings were elaborate and looked expensive. It was clear the place hadn't been cleaned in some time.

They hovered every few feet and continued through the house, going from room to room until they came upon an open doorway leading to the lower level.

Henry became increasingly nervous as they began their descent. At the bottom, they spotted the door they had seen from outside, toward the right side of the room.

They quickly took cover in the leaves of a fake, plastic tree standing in the far left corner and waited. Almost immediately, they could hear Violet's raised voice.

"What does this stone do?"

They heard Sersha's voice, but it was a small and muffled response. It was obvious that Sersha was still trapped inside the jar.

"Tell me now "princess," or you will beg for mercy before I'm through with you."

Violet's voice was somewhat different. It was colder, more sinister. It gave Henry a very different picture of her in his mind. It was an evil voice.

Just then, they saw a flash of light and the sound of a car door closing. He and Theodore exchanged looks.

The doorbell rang upstairs. It sounded far off, but its effects were instant. The room became silent as a tomb. The doorbell rang again.

"Turn off the light," hissed Violet. "They'll think no one's here."

"My car is in the drive," said Ike. "I have to answer it."

"No, you don't!" Violet argued.

There was a scuffle inside the room, and the door swung open.

Henry and Theodore watched as Ike grabbed Violet by the throat while the stranger stood by, nervously watching.

"You don't know who you're messing with, little girl. You'll do what I tell you."

Ike never looked more menacing.

"Now shut up and stay here," he snapped, flicking off the light.

Ike hurried up the steps as the doorbell rang a third time.

Henry and Theodore seized the moment and flew to the open doorway. With a snap of spark like a flash bulb, they illuminated the room as they changed size.

The light blinded Violet momentarily, giving Theodore just enough time to grab her from behind and pin her arms at her side.

"Not a word," he growled in her ear, "or you will cease to exist."

The stranger cowered in the corner, frozen in fear as Henry dashed to the glass jar and lifted it.

Sersha burst to full size. She was seething and rushed past Henry and took back her sword. She held it to Violet's throat.

"Now, who's a pathetic breed?" she whispered. "Have you forgotten who I am? I'm not just a princess; I'm a guardian of Roan. I am its protector. A warrior. A soldier. I have been trained in the way of battle. Trained to kill if necessary, to protect and preserve the sanctity of our realm."

Sersha's hand was steady. Her heart pounded as she took long, deep breaths. She was experiencing multiple emotions of an extreme nature, clearly trying to process them rationally as she held the blade.

A tiny trickle of blood rolled down Violet's neck, soiling her collar and spreading like a drop of water on a paper towel.

Violet made a gurgling sound as she struggled for words. Her eyes welled up with tears as she begged for forgiveness.

"I'm not buying it," said Sersha. "I saw how you acted at Mathilda's. You're quite a little actress, but you're not fooling anyone but yourself."

Henry stepped forward and laid his hand on Sersha's arm.

She flinched slightly as if she'd forgotten anyone else was in the room. She lowered her weapon and took a step back.

"Bind her," she said quietly, flicking on the light.

Violet tried to use that brief moment to get away, but Theodore had a firm grip on her.

Sersha picked up the stone and rapped it on the floor three times.

Chapter Eleven

A SUMMON FOR HELP

Haley woke the next morning feeling totally rested. Outside, it was raining again, and the sky was dark gray and chilly.

She got up and went to the window, looking out toward the distant mountains. Sheets of rain mostly obscured their outline.

Haley took a deep breath and sighed. The vision before her reminded her of home, and she wondered how her parents were doing and, even more, if Henry and Sersha were all right.

Roan was so beautiful in any weather, and she felt a sense of satisfaction just being here.

She cracked the window and breathed in the scent of dirt, rain, and the sweet fragrance of the millions of flowers scattered throughout the realm.

All was quiet except for the pitter-patter of raindrops against the glass. The forest floor was dark, but the lamps shone dully. Haley caught a whiff of smoke wafting from the many cottages and shops as they began a new day.

She stood at her window for almost an hour, just taking it all in, enjoying every minute. Many things went through her mind in that hour. Her entire experience with the Manwans was fulfilling for her. Haley had found purpose and a sense of belonging she never expected. She had so much to learn and knew there was much she could teach them to help them develop their species.

Haley heard a faraway gong sound, like a bell. She checked the clock. It was an unusual clock with only one hand. Morning was written at the top of the clock, and night at the bottom. The hand was precisely on the morning notch, so she knew it was very early.

She turned from the window went to the bath and climbed into the tub.

"Nice warm water and bubbles," she said to the faucet.

The tub began to fill as large pink and blue bubbles began to form. She settled back and had a nice long soak.

When she finished, she picked out a bittersweet-colored gown from her closet. It was exquisitely made. Delicate embroidery graced the bodice with fine, long silk sleeves, and the train flowed so beautifully behind her. It was backless, of course, with a wide, pale gold-colored sash around the waist. She wanted to look extra special for her prince today, and she put her hair up in a high ponytail, leaving small ringlets at her temples and down the back of her neck.

She slid on matching bittersweet slippers and checked herself in the full-length mirror.

Haley felt beautiful and looked down at her betrothal bracelet, admiring the sparkles of the rubies.

Satisfied, she left for the dining hall. She had forgotten her speech and wasn't worried about it at all. She felt confident they would solve the problems they faced, and all would be well.

Haley heard a shuffling behind her as she walked down the hall and turned to see her steward scurrying to catch up.

"Milady, milady, you mustn't go unescorted," he said uneasily. "It will be reported that I'm lacking in my duties."

Haley flashed a smile at him, and his face softened at once.

"I'm sorry. I wouldn't want to get you into trouble," she said, looping her arm around his.

He wore a big smile the rest of the way.

The dining hall was mostly empty. Haley took this time to walk around the room and check out all the beautiful tables.

The brownies did a fabulous job making things special. Vases filled with fragrant coral roses graced the white linen-covered tabletops and the usual gem-filled glass bowls.

The place settings were simple yet elegant. The white china plates were square in shape, accentuated by gold utensils and crystal goblets.

The usual seats had been replaced by high-back chairs with plush cushions in coral, and gold candelabrums favored the center of each table, gleaming in the flickering candlelight.

The dark, overcast skies gave the entire room ambiance, making everything feel cozy but cool.

The dining hall had three great fireplaces, one in the center of each wall, except for the columned entryway.

Haley ordered one of the brownies, walking through with a tray full of crystal salt and pepper shakers to light fires in all of the fireplaces to take off the chill.

She went to the covered court just inside the columns and watched the rain pelting off the leaves of the trees and took in the woodsy aroma.

As she took pleasure in the scene before her, fairies began to arrive in twos and threes, landing and hurrying inside.

The brownies had stacks of white towels ready on the long marble tables that lined the entry.

Haley immediately noticed the calm demeanor the fairies displayed as they congregated in front of the fires, and she marveled again at the control of the given gems.

More fairies continued to arrive and bowed to her as they landed. She was taken aback by this and wondered why they would pay her such tribute. Maybe it was because she was betrothed to the prince.

Haley cocked her head for a moment, feeling a presence behind her. Turning to see Valian standing there watching her, she smiled and curtsied.

"Good morning, Prince Valian," she said playfully.

He looked valiant, tall, strong, and commanding. His pale blue eyes had a sparkle in them, and the smile he displayed caused his dimples to stand out on his rugged face.

Haley held her breath as she looked at his masculine frame.

He wore a dark gray silk tunic with a silver sash around his waist, and his silver armlet was studded with emeralds. He also bore his sword upon his hip, which Haley found unusual.

"You are a vision," he said as she approached.

"Thank you," she replied.

He took her bejeweled hand and kissed it gently.

She blushed, and he chuckled at her apparent shyness.

"Are you ready?" he asked, taking her arm.

"Absolutely," she answered, as they approached the head table.

He pulled out her chair for her, and they sat together, waiting for the room to fill.

A few minutes later, dozens of trays were brought out, and the fairies began to load their plates.

The room got quiet as they waited for the prince.

Valian stood and addressed the group.

"Good morning. Thank you all for coming," he said, looking around the room. "Let us share in this meal and rejoice for a new day."

There were nods of agreement as they began to eat.

The room buzzed with conversation and laughter all through breakfast, and everyone was comfortable and at ease when they were finished.

As soon as the tables were cleared, Valian stood again.

"Again, thank you for coming this morning. First, I would like to let you know how much I appreciate each of you for your service and dedication to the royal court and the whole of Roan. When Haley and I arrived back from our retreat, I was disturbed to hear of the anarchy rampant within the city."

A low whispering and mumbling broke out across the room.

Valian raised his hand for quiet.

"However," he continued, "we have discovered the culprit behind the confusion. The removal of your given gems has caused each of you to fall prey to a host of emotions."

The look of shock was almost humorous to Haley. It was like telling a group of second graders they could have cake and ice cream for breakfast from now on, and she smiled at them as Valian continued.

"We have learned that the given gem has a protective property that has shielded you from what we are normally supposed to possess. I am quite certain that from the beginning, before the rift, we all experienced emotion much like the humans."

The response in the room was shock, bewilderment, and disbelief.

Valian paused as the group digested the news. Many hands were raised with questions.

"I'll take questions at the end of the meeting," Valian interrupted. "Needless to say, none of you knew how to respond to or process these feelings. That is why you reacted the way you did. Since I ordered everyone to put their gems back on, things have calmed down considerably, as you can see."

"I am going to give you all the options. You can continue to wear your given gems as you wish. If you decide you want to remove them and take on the challenge of a whole new experience, there will be no objection; in fact, I encourage it. I don't know if you know this, but when I was injured in the Spicewood realm, my given gem was lost, and I began to experience an emotion I never dreamed of. Some of it was frightening, but mostly, it was fascinating and wondrous. I encourage all of you to consider it carefully before you decide."

"Haley, who is the expert on emotion will be here to teach you not only what you're feeling, but how to deal with it, to process it and benefit from it."

The room was quiet for a while, the fairies considered all they had just learned.

"Think it over, and if you decide to remove your gems, you will be required to make your mark," said Valian, as he unrolled a long scroll.

He mounted the scroll to a tall easel and placed a quill and ink on a small table next to it.

"Haley and I are to be present when any of you decide to accept this great responsibility. Haley, have you any words of wisdom?"

Haley stood and rose in the air a few inches.

"Prince Valian's words are true. It is a great responsibility to live with emotion and challenge. It is not an easy thing to learn. It takes dedication and practice on your part, not to mention diligence, and as the prince said, it can be scary but the benefits will be infinite. Emotion will help you grow stronger and give you confidence as you learn to harness its qualities. And like my betrothed," she said, giving Valian an affectionate smile, "I encourage you to try. If you find it something you would rather decline, that's okay too."

Haley took her seat, blushing slightly.

Valian smiled as he caressed her wing.

Suddenly, Valian cocked his head, and the strangest look crossed his face; surprise, anxiety, and curiosity all in one look.

Haley looked at him questioningly, suddenly afraid but not knowing why she felt that way.

He reached into the pocket of his tunic and pulled out a glowing, blue stone. He began tossing it from one hand to the other like a hot potato. He quickly looked at Haley.

She realized at once something was wrong. Henry and Sersha were in trouble. Her heart began to pound, and she stood up nervously.

Valian looked at the crowd of curious onlookers.

"Haley and I have urgent business. Everyone, keep your gems on until our return. That's an order."

He turned to Haley.

"Let's go," he said seriously.

They hurried to the open archways. Valian took Haley by the arm.

"You hold on tight. We must make haste."

She wrapped her arm around his and held on, not knowing what to expect.

They took off at breakneck speed with a great burst of his wings.

Haley glanced back at the quickly disappearing palace and the fairies gathered in the doorways.

She had never traveled so fast in her life and had no idea Valian was so powerful. His jaw was clenched, and his muscles flexed with every flap of the wing.

Haley looked ahead as the land sped past in a blur, out of the rain and into sunny skies, until they slowed as they approached a large cyclone of swirling leaves.

Valian took them straight into the vortex, and they disappeared.

Haley squealed as they entered the mass. Leaves flew around them everywhere in a fury. It was windy and dusty and almost violent. She didn't dare open her mouth to ask questions and held onto Valian's arm more tightly than ever.

They emerged as quickly as they entered into the dawn of the other side.

Valian looked around quickly as Hilda blasted out of thin air just ahead of them. She hovered on her broom, scanning her surroundings. Her hair was a sight. It stood straight out as if electrified, like she'd put her finger in a light socket.

"This way," she said, flying up over a pine forest.

Valian and Haley followed, flying just over the treetops. They crested a large hill and paused as they gazed down at Ike's house below.

Hilda spotted something and flew quickly to the edge of the property.

Haley's mouth dropped open as Estelle and Troy flew toward them.

"Blessed be," said Hilda.

"Blessed be," Estelle answered as the sisters hugged.

Estelle flew to Valian and Haley, giving them a quick hug.

"What's going on?" Hilda asked.

"Shh," Estelle whispered, pointing to the front of the house.

Haley gasped.

"That's my mother," she exclaimed, trying to keep her voice down. "What is she doing here?" she asked fearfully. "And where are Henry and Sersha?"

Estelle quickly explained what had happened and the fact that Henry and Theodore had disappeared into the chimney and hadn't come out. Now Carol was ringing the doorbell.

"She was supposed to bring your father with her," Estelle said anxiously.

The group watched silently as Ike opened the door. They could hear words being exchanged as they quietly flew closer.

" . . . just wondering if you have seen them. They didn't come home last night, and I'm worried. I mean, they often go camping, but they always tell me when they're going," Carol was saying.

"No, no, I haven't," Ike answered. "If I see . . . "

Ike suddenly looked past Carol in surprise.

Carol turned to look just as Valian plowed into Ike, sending him through the door and crashing into the middle of the floor.

Carol let out a shriek as the others flew past her into the house.

Valian stood over Ike, his sword an inch from Ike's chest.

"Remember me?" he thundered.

Recognition was written all over Ike's face. He opened his mouth to reply but no words came. He just sat there white-faced, afraid to move.

"Where are Henry and Sersha?" Haley demanded.

Ike's lips moved but without sound as he glanced toward the other room.

"Henry! Sersha!" Haley yelled.

"Haley?" Henry's voice echoed up the stairs.

"Yes. Where are you?"

"In the basement!"

"Watch him," Valian instructed.

"With pleasure," said Estelle.

"You think fairies are bad? Try witches," Hilda said, with a mischievous grin. "Just try."

Valian and Haley left the room for the basement.

"Are you alright?" Haley called.

"Just fab," Henry answered.

A huge smile came over Haley's face at Henry's sarcasm.

They descended the stairs and stood at the bottom in shock at the sight before them.

"Now, why doesn't this surprise me?" Haley said, in disgust.

Valian stood there, his jaw locked and a look of contempt on his face.

"You disappoint me, Violet," he said quietly.

Theodore stood there grinning. He still had her in a bear hold.

"Prince Valian . . . this is all a mistake. I came here . . . " Violet began.

"You came here to interfere, to cause trouble, to come between me and my love," Valian interrupted. "You will pay for your betrayal."

"Please, my Lord . . . "

"Silence her," Valian commanded.

Sersha waved her hand, and instantly, Violet's voice was gone. She hurried over to Valian and Haley and threw her arms around them.

"I'm so glad you're alright," she said, happily.

She turned to Henry and embraced him.

"Thank you for stopping me," she whispered into his ear, kissing him on the cheek.

Just then, the stranger bolted, white-faced and petrified, flying up the stairs. Valian let him pass.

"Come, let's get upstairs," he suggested.

Once they reached the landing, Haley and Valian began to chuckle.

Hilda and Estelle had Ike bound and gagged as a feather tickled his face. He lay on the floor in torment, trying to scratch his nose. The sisters were sitting on the sofa watching as Ike entertained them.

"Are you finished entertaining yourselves?" Valian inquired, his smile infused with warmth and affection.

"No, we're just getting started," said Hilda with glee.

"Let him go," Valian instructed.

"Let him go?" Henry exclaimed. "Aren't you gonna punish him?"

"No," Valian answered. "We cannot interfere in human affairs. This is your world not ours. It is one of our most sacred laws."

"But . . . " Henry began.

"Valian is right," Sersha interrupted. "He cannot be touched on this side. You, on the other hand . . . " she said, walking up to Violet, "can be punished by us no matter what side you're on."

The relish in her voice made the others give her a curious look.

"Ahem."

They turned. Carol stood in the doorway. Her face was pale.

"Mom!" Haley cried, rushing toward her.

Carol was speechless as her daughter threw her arms around her. She stood quite still for a moment, not sure if it was all real. She finally let out the breath she was holding and embraced her.

"Oh, Mom! I've so much to tell you," Haley said excitedly.

"First things first, Haley," Valian said gently.

He turned to Theodore and Troy.

"Take her back to Roan. Check her into the psych ward in the infirmary and keep her locked up until our return."

"Here, use my gem," said Sersha, taking off her sapphire necklace.

She handed it to Theodore as Troy had his hands full.

"Speaking of gems," said Henry. "I believe he . . . " he said, motioning toward Ike who was still on the floor not daring to move, "has something that belongs to you, Prince Valian."

Valian looked at Henry questioningly.

Ike seized the moment and dashed out the door like his butt was on fire.

The others started for the door when they heard a sound like sticks cracking in a fire followed by a loud yelp.

Valian dashed across the porch and saw Ike all tangled up in a tree. A tall willow stood smack dab in the middle of the yard. Its branches wrapped around Ike so tightly he couldn't move a muscle.

Henry and Haley began to laugh.

"Ruena? Is that you?" Valian asked astonished.

A long mournful wail echoed down the valley.

"It is I, Prince Valian, Princess Sersha," she wailed sorrowfully.

She bent low in a bow, all the while keeping Ike tight in her grip.

"Well I'll be," said Hilda in wonder.

"Good work Ruena," said Henry chuckling.

"Well this is a turn of events," Valian replied, walking up to the great willow.

He turned to Henry.

"What am I looking for?"

"Your given gem," Henry replied.

Delicately and with a sense of purpose, Valian reached into Ike's shirt pocket, to retrieved the diamond necklace that rested within.

"And the map," Henry added.

Valian checked and found the map rolled up like a scroll in Ike's back pocket.

"Don't ever let me catch you on our side. I may not be able to touch you here, but in our world all bets are off. Do you understand me?" Valian asked in a low menacing voice.

Ike tried to nod but couldn't.

"Let him go, Ruena," he instructed. "Meet us back in the outskirts and we will seek council together."

Ruena wailed mournfully and let go of Ike.

He rolled from her branches like a yo-yo on a string.

Theodore and Troy took off, Violet between them squirming like a worm on a hook.

Haley smiled and turned toward the prince. She glanced toward her mother, her heart beating fast.

"Mom, I would like to introduce you to Prince Valian; guardian and protector of Roan."

Carol approached Valian cautiously as if afraid she'd make a mistake and insult the prince. She held out her hand and made a shaky, feeble attempt at a curtsy.

Valian's eyes sparkled and he smiled that smile Haley was so fond of. He took Carol's hand and kissed it.

"I can see where Haley gets her beauty," he said softly.

Carol blushed and began to giggle like a school girl.

"And Mom, this is Valian's sister Sersha; Princess and guardian of Roan."

Sersha walked right up to Carol and startled her with a big hug.

"Haley and Henry are our heroes," Sersha said, smiling brightly. "They have been instrumental in saving us in so many ways. You should be proud."

Carol still had a look on her face as if she were numb struck.

"I . . . I can't believe this. I see it, but can't believe it."

She looked from one to the other in awe.

"Perhaps we should take leave of this place to more suitable surroundings," Valian suggested, glancing at Ike.

"Oh, yes. We can go to our place," Carol replied amazed.

"What do you say, Mom? Would you like to fly?" Henry asked with a grin.

Carol's eyes grew wide.

"Y. . . Yes . . . " she said excitedly. "What about my car?"

"Oh we'll take care of that," said Hilda cheerfully.

"Well . . . okay," Carol agreed, a little leery.

"Okay then," said Henry, taking her by the arm.

Haley took her other arm.

"You ready?" she asked, smiling at her mother.

"Y . . . yes."

The twins slowly rose into the air.

"Ah . . . ah . . . " Carol stuttered, nervously.

"It's alright Mom," said Henry. "Here we go!"

Carol let out a squeal that echoed across the valley as the twins picked up speed.

"This is great!" she cried, as they crested the tree line and zipped out of sight, with Valian and Sersha close behind.

Hilda and Estelle watched them disappear, wearing big smiles. Hilda turned and gave Ike the evil eye.

"You'll mind your Ps and Qs if you know what's good for you," she growled, as Ike stood there as if paralyzed.

"Yeah, we'll have to sic Ruena on you," Estelle chuckled as she opened the door to the Miles' minivan.

"Come on, let's get out of here," she said.

Hilda climbed into the passenger seat.

"This will be a new experience for me," she said excitedly.

Estelle slammed on the gas, and they peeled out of Ike's driveway, spraying gravel and screaming, "Hee!" all the way to the road.

Ike stood frozen as he watched Ruena slowly turn toward the Kootenai River, wailing mournfully as she went. Finally, he gathered himself together, stormed up the steps, and slammed the door behind him.

Anyone out and about at such an early hour would have heard excited squeals and the familiar, long, mournful wailing that morning.

As they flew toward the estate, Carol couldn't contain herself, squealing and laughing all the way.

They landed at the back kitchen door.

Carol stood there, her legs shaking.

"That was exhilarating!" she exclaimed. "Well, come on in everyone."

Minutes later, Hilda and Estelle skidded to a halt in the driveway, hurried in, and went right to get some breakfast started. The rest of the group gathered at the butcher block table.

Carol was out of breath from all the excitement and kept shaking her head in disbelief. She looked at her children in wonder and couldn't stop staring at Valian and Sersha.

Gazing upon the prince and princess with an appreciative expression, she uttered, "You two, are undeniably and extraordinarily beautiful."

Her eyes were wide and her face flushed.

"So . . ." she began, "tell me everything from the beginning."

They sat for hours as they retold the story of the land of Wisen.

Haley, Henry, Valian, and Sersha sat fanning their wings as they enjoyed a wonderful breakfast.

Carol was amazed as she watched Hilda and Estelle prepare breakfast as things flew through the air. It was a comfortable, laid back atmosphere as they laughed and giggled. There were gasps of surprise and suspense from Carol in all the right places.

The sun had come up, warming the kitchen and making everyone relax. The twins were all smiles as they watched their mother's reactions.

Haley sat quietly, enjoying the conversation. The hard part was coming up when she would have to tell Carol about the betrothal between her and Valian. She was worried.

Valian looked over at her. He seemed to sense what she was thinking. He too, sat quietly, listening to the others.

Soon, Henry and Sersha became quiet and looked at Haley and the prince expectantly.

Carol looked around at them all.

"What?" she asked, curiously.

"Well . . . I've saved the best for last," said Haley, looking intently at her mother.

Everyone smiled encouragingly.

Haley held out her right wrist. Her bracelet sparkled.

"Oh, that's beautiful," Carol exclaimed. "Where . . . "

"It's a betrothal bracelet," Haley interrupted.

"A betro . . . "

"Valian and I are engaged," she blurted out.

Her heart was beating a hundred miles an hour as she watched her mother's expression of shock.

Carol's mouth dropped open.

"Valian asked me to marry him not long ago," Haley continued, "and I accepted."

Carol was about to respond.

"Let me finish," Haley said quietly. "Manwan law states that once a couple is betrothed, they cannot marry for three years, so as you can see, this will be a long engagement."

Carol sat there silently. She looked from Haley to Valian.

Do you love her?" she asked, in a most serious voice.

"With all my heart," he answered.

"I will give you my blessing under one condition. Haley, you will finish school and will only be allowed to visit the other side during the summer months. Speaking of school, I believe you two have missed a few days already?" she smiled. Once you graduate, you can decide whether you want to marry."

Haley opened her mouth, but Carol interrupted her.

"Let me finish. You can remain engaged . . . "

Haley let out a relieved sigh.

"But, you must have to have your father's consent," she said, talking to Haley, but looking at Valian.

"I wouldn't have it any other way," said Valian, with a soft smile.

"Very well," said Carol.

The whole table was all smiles.

Hilda and Estelle got up to refill everyone's tea.

"So, why did you go to Ike's by yourself?" Estelle asked, changing the subject.

"I woke Paul and told him what was going on, and he said I was having a dream and to go back to sleep, so I went without him. Speak of the devil," said Carol, as an upstairs door closed loudly. "I think it would be best if he didn't see your wings," she chuckled. "He'd think he was dreaming."

Everyone shrouded their wings as Paul came plopping down the stairs. He shuffled into the kitchen, rubbing his left eye. His hair was disheveled, and he was still in his pajamas.

"Man, I must have been tired to sleep for so long . . . " he stopped when he saw the group staring at him.

"Hi," he said, looking at everyone. "Carol, why didn't you tell me we had company?" he asked, walking toward her.

Carol flashed him a smile.

"Honey, sit down, and I'll tell you all about it."

For the rest of the morning the group repeated the story, with all the laughter and suspense as before.

Paul took a liking to Valian and Sersha at once and was as bewildered as Carol had been, and when the wings came out, the look on his face was priceless.

All in all, it was a wonderful morning getting acquainted, and when it came to Haley's betrothal, Paul was in complete agreement with Carol.

"I just can't believe that the Bonners are truly alive and well, living in your world," said Carol, getting up for more tea. "It would be fascinating to be able to meet them."

"That's a marvelous idea," Estelle agreed.

"Let's invite them back for a visit," Carol continued. "They could see their old homestead and how things have changed over the years."

"I know," said Haley, "perhaps we could have them back for the autumn festival?"

"Yeah!" Henry agreed.

"I'll see to it personally," Hilda chimed in, "and I also think it would be in your best interest to visit the land of Wisen," she said, looking at Paul and Carol. "You really should see where the twins have spent so much time. It truly is a wondrous place."

"I agree," said Valian. "You will need to meet our mother . . . " he paused. "I almost forgot in all this excitement; she is still missing."

The group was somber and quiet.

"We're just gonna have to put our heads together," said Haley, optimistically. "We've already been through some rough times and have come out of it with success."

Valian nodded.

"Yes, we shall be victorious. I swear and make a solemn vow here, and now, I will search to the ends of the earth until I find her, and bring her home safely, and bring those responsible to justice, including Reed if indeed he is involved," he proclaimed, lifting his hand in the air in front of Haley.

She gave him an enthusiastic high five. He turned to Sersha and slapped her hand. Everyone gave each other high fives, and the smiles were abundant.

Ike stormed through the living room and into the kitchen. He was livid. He paced back and forth, his mind going in a million different directions. He was furious about what had just happened and at himself for not seeing it coming.

He slowed down and sat on a tall stool in front of the granite countertop bar, deep in thought.

The house was quiet except for a soft humming sound that grew louder and louder until he cocked his head to listen.

He saw movement out of the corner of his eye and turned to see Violet standing right behind him with a huge grin on her face. It startled him, and he almost fell off the stool.

"How did you get away?" he stammered.

"Those idiots," she answered with a smirk on her face. "Right as we got to the portal, those boneheads changed size. What for is beyond me. It didn't cross their minds that I wouldn't change size, and I knocked them both out before they could enter the portal," she laughed wickedly. "Then, then I tied them up and tossed them through."

Ike gave her an evil smile.

"I'm impressed," he chuckled.

"We need to leave here now," she said. "It won't be long before they wake up and sound the alarm."

"Right," said Ike, getting up. "Once we get to the other side, I'm going to need to find another given gem."

"That should be easy," said Violet, "since a bunch of those Manwans have taken them off."

Ike raised an eyebrow.

"Really? I'll just go and steal one then."

"How are you possibly going to do that?" Violet asked, sarcastically.

Ike held out a handful of dwindle drops.

She smiled.

"Well done. And how did you get your hands on those?"

"None of your business," Ike snapped, leering at her. "Don't forget, I'm in charge here."

A defiant look crossed her face.

"You may be able to shrink, but you can't fly, idiot."

Ike looked as if he were about to strike her, then changed his mind.

"You didn't think of that, did you?" she sneered.

"Watch yourself," Ike replied, pointing his finger at her.

The power struggle between the two was obvious. Both craved power and riches and seemed willing to do anything to get them.

Violet began tapping her foot.

"Are you coming?" she demanded.

"Yes," he growled.

The sun had just risen when they left Ike's place. They walked towards the nearest portal since Ike couldn't fly, and they argued the entire way.

They arrived at a spot on the banks of the Kootenai River directly across the valley from the Miles' estate.

"Where is it?" Ike asked. "Should I eat one of these drops now?"

Violet had a sly look on her face.

"No, not yet; just as soon as we're through, you can eat it. The portal is right here."

Ike looked but couldn't see anything and threw her a suspicious look.

"It's alright, you moron," she said, rolling her eyes. "Now come on, take my hand."

Her sarcasm made Ike believe she was on the up and up, and he grasped her hand.

"Now, when I say go, we'll jump forward."

Ike nodded.

"Ready, set, go!"

Ike jumped.

Violet let go just as he was sucked into the vortex, and she hovered there, listening to his fading screams with a devious look of utter satisfaction.

About the Author

Elizabeth Rymer Patterson, a spellbinding author from Florida, invites readers on an enchanting journey into the magical realms of the *Bonners' Fairy* series. With a childhood love for fairy tales and a passion for nature, Elizabeth's storytelling seamlessly blends fantasy and reality. Her tales transport readers to whimsical landscapes where fairies dance, and magic intertwines with everyday life. Join Elizabeth on a magical adventure through the pages of her *Bonners' Fairy* books, where ordinary moments transform into extraordinary wonders.

Bonners' Fairy Series

Book One
The Legend Begins

Book Two
A New Kind of Battle

Book Three
Mischief and Mayhem

Book Four
Sailing Toward Destiny

Book Five
Secrets and Spies

Book Six
Caroline Belle and the Curse of a Blue Moon
(To be released in 2025)

Resources

Website
https://www.bonnersfairy.com

Facebook
www.facebook.com/BonnersFairy

www.ingramcontent.com/pod-product-compliance
Lightning Source LLC
Chambersburg PA
CBHW040826010826
48978CB00012BB/619